YOU HAVE CHOSEN

YOU HAVE CHOSEN

Denise Robins

CHIVERS

British Library Cataloguing in Publication Data available

This Large Print edition published by BBC Audiobooks Ltd, Bath, 2008.
Published by arrangement with the Author's estate.

U.K. Hardcover ISBN 978 1 405 64420 4
U.K. Softcover   ISBN 978 1 405 64421 1

Printed and bound in Great Britain by
Antony Rowe Ltd., Chippenham, Wiltshire

'You have chosen and clung to the
Chance they sent you
Life sweet as perfume . . .
But will it now one day in
Heaven repent you?'

'Triumph of Time'
SWINBURNE.

CHAPTER ONE

It seemed to Toni the longest day she had ever spent.

For September, it was unusually hot. An 'Indian Summer' can be lovely. But in town it is apt to become singularly trying for workers in small shops. And 'Violette's' was surely the smallest and stuffiest shop in Shaftesbury Avenue? So thought Toni, as she ran up and down the basement stairs, selling clothes. Cheap, shoddy clothes which she hated just about as much as she hated the whole atmosphere of the place.

The buxom, hard-driving woman who was her employer kept her girls hard at it from nine in the morning until half past six at night. There were two others besides Toni. Helena, the tallest and darkest, was a mannequin.

Toni shared a flat with Helena. Sometimes she wondered which one of them worked the harder. It was exhausting in this weather to put on dresses and drag them off again hour after hour. Equally so to take this gown off a hook or that coat from the cupboard and enter into endless arguments and discussions with tiresome customers.

Madame was not very pleased, either, if the customer retired having purchased nothing. When that happened, instead of blaming the fact upon her own choice of garments, Madame invariably cursed the girl who had not put through the sale.

This evening, as Toni washed her hands and powdered her nose in the tiny cloakroom at the back of the shop, she wondered whether life must go on like this for ever.

She was young. She was pretty, and passionately fond of life and all that it offered. And it appeared to offer nothing at the moment but drudgery. Time and time again, Toni had tried to get other work and failed. And she could not afford to be out of a job, because, except for an old aunt in Cornwall whom she never saw, and a few cousins who had not the least interest in her, she was alone in the world.

A year ago, after the death of her mother which had left her penniless, she had been offered work at 'Violette's' and seized it gladly, because she was on the verge of being turned out of the tiny two-roomed flat in Earls Court which was her home. Later, Helena, with whom she had made friends at the shop, elected to share the expenses of the flat with her.

Helena was a queer, secretive girl a few years older than Toni. She had good points. She could be very gay and amusing. But she had a side which Toni discovered shortly after they started living together. A side which she could not pretend to admire. Ugly,

2

greedy, Helena was insatiable for admiration. Ungenerous in many of her ideas about life and love. Yet in Toni's eyes, Helena was lucky. She had something to look forward to in the future. And Toni had nothing.

Helena had been engaged for the last twelve months. Her fiancé, Nicholas Brendan, was madly in love with her, but because he had no money they had not been able to marry at once. Almost immediately after their engagement, he had been offered a partnership in a silver-fox farm out in the South of France, and since then had been there, away from Helena. The farm was not paying sufficiently to enable him to support a wife. In any case, his contract did not permit him to marry during the first year. So Helena Lane, in the same impecunious and orphaned position as Toni, continued her job in 'Violette's'.

And for the last few months she had been as discontented and unhappy as Toni. Discontent had not a similar reaction upon Toni as it had on Helena. Toni grew quiet and introspective. Helena went into flaming, angry moods which made her snatch at every little chance of gaiety that life offered. Sometimes Toni was horrified by Helena's lack of constancy. One moment she would dash off a love-letter to her fiancé assuring him of her fidelity, and the next moment she would be dining and dancing with any young man who asked her.

Indeed, there had been many days when Toni turned from her friend in disgust, and wondered what Nicholas Brendon, out there on his farm to make a home for Helena, would think if he knew what she was like.

And now there was a new interest in Helena's life. No ordinary young man without means, ready to give her a dinner in Soho or an evening in the cheap seats of a cinema. But a rich member of 'Society' who would one day come into a title. A mere boy, just 'down' from the Varsity, who had 'fallen' for Helena's magnificent figure and rich gipsy colouring.

It was not really Toni's business what Helena did and she rarely bothered to criticize her, nor protest when Helena jeered at her for being stupid and stand-offish in her own dealings with men. She called Toni incurably romantic, and Toni let her laugh. But there was something to be said for romance, whatever Helena thought.

Curiously enough, the one thing which Toni could not tolerate was Helena's callous attitude towards her fiancé.

Toni had never met Nicholas Brendon. But she knew a great deal about him. Helena, when in a communicative mood, liked to talk intimately of him and even read some of his letters aloud. Letters that seemed to Toni the loveliest things in the world, for they were the outpourings of a man's sincere, honest heart. A man who really loved Helena and believed in her.

Helena's romance was, in a queer way, also Toni's. She moved in its aura and waited for those letters with the French postmark even more eagerly than Helena waited for them. At moments, ludicrous though it seemed, Toni had to admit that she was far more excited than Helena when they came home and found one of those foreign-looking envelopes with the blue stamp, lying on the mat. Another love-letter for Helena. Nothing for Toni. Photographs of Nicholas in the bedroom which she shared with Helena, and in the little sitting-room. She knew every line of his face, was familiar with his smile, the idiosyncrasies of his nature, as Helena had described them to her.

This hot September evening Toni put on her hat, found Helena and walked with her from the shop. Outside the heat was almost greater, flung up from the concrete pavements. It seemed no cooler now when it was sundown than it had been at midday.

'Heavens!' said Toni. 'I am exhausted. Aren't you?'

'Absolutely done,' said Helena. 'Thank God Bobby is driving me down to the river for dinner. We shall bathe and get cool.'

Toni made no reply. She was not going to tell Helena that she was lucky. Nor congratulate her on the fact that Bobby Deane was heir to a quarter of a million and ran a

Rolls-Bentley and could afford to give Helena exactly the sort of time she wanted. There was that wretched boy out there in France whose one aim and object was to send for Helena and make her his wife.

Toni said:

'I wouldn't mind the heat if one hadn't to work so hard. I don't suppose it'll last. The papers said this morning that it would soon break. It isn't really seasonable. I expect we shall have a raw, cold October and then we'll grumble because we can't get warm.'

Helena Lane stepped on to a bus with her friend. She was hardly listening to Toni. She was looking through her heavily blacked eyelashes at a young man who had admired the slim roundness of her ankle as she boarded the bus.

She adored admiration, even from strangers, and was always rather pleased to be seen about with Toni. They were such a good foil for each other. Toni, so small and fair, with very little colour, especially in this heat, faded, Helena felt, into insignificance beside her own glowing beauty. Although at times she admitted that Toni could look lovely. But she was rather a little fool in Helena's estimation. Too full of ideals and principles. Very boring to Helena. Her Nick had the same sort of outlook on life. She had learned that since her engagement. And a virtuous young man without cash was really not so acceptable as a young cad like Bobby with his thousands. (A Cad, by the way, whom she fully intended to land in the matrimonial net before she was finished with him.)

The two girls reached Earls Court and their two-roomed flatlet in the big converted house which was not far from the Underground. The rooms were cruelly hot in this weather. Both girls, gasping, rushed to open all the windows which had been left shut.

It was by no means a modern or luxurious home. The house had been converted ten years ago. The kitchenette was without a refrigerator and the dilapidated bathroom had an old-fashioned geyser. The furniture was out of date, although good, solid stuff which had belonged to Toni's mother. Toni did not dislike it here, because it was the home in which she had once been happy with a much-loved parent. Not that she did not sigh for something more. But Helena frankly loathed it and accepted it only because it was a cheap deal for her, living here with Toni. She was supposed to share the work with Toni, but it was the younger girl who was left to do the major portion.

Helena was a genius at slipping out of her responsibilities with the best possible excuse.

She knew perfectly well that Toni disapproved of her general conduct, but she also knew that Toni was generous and kind-hearted. She could always work the 'sympathy

7

stuff' on Toni when she wanted to.

She did it tonight. Bobby was expecting her at their meeting-place in the West End, in an hour's time. She must get a bath and dress at once.

She said:

'Toni darling, my head aches frightfully. Would you be an angel and make a cup of tea while I slip into the bath?'

Toni gave a faint smile.

Innumerable were Helena's headaches and demands for 'cups of tea'.

'All right.'

Toni walked across the sitting-room. On a table by the window, beside a vase of half-dead chrysanthemums which she had bought as a great extravagance at the beginning of the week, stood a photograph. An enlarged snapshot taken out in France of Nicholas Brendon.

Helena, slipping out of her dress and putting on a cretonne wrapper, looked through the doorway and grinned at Toni.

'I love the way you moon over old Nick's picture!' she exclaimed.

A slight colour rose in Toni's cheeks, but she continued to look at the photograph.

'Don't you ever think of him yourself, Helena?'

'When I have to. I answered one of his letters yesterday, didn't I?'

'One of them,' said Toni slowly. 'One—out

of his every three.'

Helena went into the bathroom, lit the geyser, turned on the bath and shouted to Toni through the sound of the running water:

'He's lucky to get that, when I'm so busy.'

Toni, unusually truculent and argumentative, called back:

'Well, you're engaged to him, aren't you?'

'That doesn't say I'm in love with him.'

Toni was shocked. It was the first time Helena had actually voiced that sentiment. Helena added:

'Anyhow, Nick's across the Channel, and farther than that. And he never seems to be able to raise the cash to send for me. Nor get out of his contract about not marrying. And why should a girl waste her life? I shall be twenty-four next month, and women don't get younger or prettier. Bobby thinks I'm the cat's whiskers, and I'm dipping them in the cream while I can! Take it from me, my angel, if I can get Bobby to propose, it's the end between Nick and me.'

After that there came a great deal of splashing and singing from the bathroom.

Toni stood silent, looking at the photograph of the man who was having such a raw deal. She thought of all the months he must have worked with an ideal in his mind. His ideal of Helena. What shock and bitterness it would be to him, if Helena let him down.

How *could* she? How could any girl be so

9

mean, so disloyal? Somehow, all that was most romantic in Toni's sensitive heart came to the fore whenever she thought about Nicholas or looked at his pictured-face.

It was a face which had a strange attraction for her. The enlarged snapshot showed him standing against a palm tree. He had been snapped while down in Mentone on a day's holiday. Toni was fascinated by the strength and grace of the man. Six-foot-one. Helena admitted that he was superbly good-looking. The brilliant sunshine of the Riviera crinkled the corners of his eyes. Rather dare-devil eyes. Helena said that Nick used to be a devil with women, but that he had never wanted to marry one until he had met her. But because he had no money and could not offer her an immediate brilliant future, so far as she was concerned, the 'devilment' had lost its attraction.

Toni turned away from the photograph and walked into the kitchenette to put on the kettle. Why worry about Nicholas Brendon and what Helena chose to do? Yet she could not stop doing so. She had been so long concerned with their engagement that it seemed part of her own life. She could not bear the thought of the disappointment awaiting him. He seemed so much too good for that.

'If only I had had Helena's chance!' Toni thought, and then laughed to herself, secretly ashamed. She was half in love with another girl's lover whom she had never even met. In love with his face and with all those letters which he had written, so many of which she had heard. She had not really wanted to hear them. In her opinion, they were sacred to Helena alone. But to Helena nothing was sacred, and because Nick's words fed her vanity, she liked Toni to see them. Sometimes she even thought that Helena took a sadistic pleasure in rousing envy in the heart of the girl who had no man to write in such a way to her.

If Nick Brendon had written those things to her, how she would have adored it, Toni thought, *and* him. She would never have looked at another man. She would have waited for him for years.

Only this morning, a letter had come. All day Toni had remembered a certain paragraph which had been carelessly quoted by Helena.

You don't know how lonely it is out here. My partner's still away in Canada and sometimes I feel I shall go mad if I can't have you with me soon. I want you so terribly. I live and work only for you. You're my life itself. Helena, I wonder if you can possibly love me as much as I love you. If you were here tonight, I think I should die with your lips against my mouth . . .

Words with a thrill that had run like a live wire through Toni, even though they left untouched the girl for whom they were intended.

She heard Helena letting the water out of the bath and hurried to make the tea. Later, when the two girls were sitting together, Toni said suddenly:

'Helena, you must be crazy. You know Nick worships you. You couldn't be so cruel as to give him up, even if Bobby Deane does come up to scratch and suggest marriage.'

Helena blew a cloud of smoke into the air.

'Don't be a sentimental idiot, Toni. And make up your mind to this. If Bobby comes up to scratch, Nick's off the map. It's only the money I want. Love is grand in theory but it's no good in practice.'

'But you're wrong! Without love, life is worth absolutely nothing.'

'Yet you've turned down two men since I've lived with you,' said Helena.

'I didn't care in the least for either of them.'

'You're very particular. I really think it's a pity, Toni, that it isn't you rather than I who became engaged to Nick. He likes women to be all soft and sweet. He used to get furious with me because I am what he called "hard and tantalizing". You shall answer Nick's last letter for me if you like.'

'I shall do nothing of the sort. And I think you're a little brute, Helena,' Toni said hotly, her face flushing scarlet.

Helena laughed. Toni walked out of the room into their bedroom. She felt exasperated with Helena and with life.

A pity that she was not engaged to Nick, Helena had said. Perhaps it was. She believed she might well have loved a man like Nicholas Brendon. And Helena did not care a damn for him. Oh, why was life so tangled—so upside-down?

Toni felt suddenly very lonely and depressed. She knew that when she loved, she would love utterly and generously. But until she met the right man she must continue to be alone. There was little to look forward to, hard work during the day at the shop, and lonely evenings in the flat, since Helena was so often out.

Tonight, after Helena had left the flat, Toni stood in front of her mirror looking wistfully at her reflection. Men told her that she was beautiful. The mirror told her so, too. She was not so striking as Helena. But she was slim and exquisitely built, from the primrose-fair head to the slender ankles. Her large, passionate eyes were a rare golden hazel under ink-black lashes. The narrow 'plucked' brows were like delicate crescent lines. The tender mouth was a red, half-opened flower. She had beauty. She had charm. She could be amusing and gay—as gay as Helena. But life offered her nothing because she could not take her pleasures

13

promiscuously where she found them. It seemed a little cruel.

That night, Toni slept badly. Restless in heart and soul. All night she dreamt vividly of another girl's love—of Nick Brendon, smiling at her as he smiled from his photograph. In her dreams she heard him say to her the words which he had written in his letter to Helena:

If you were here tonight, I think I would die with your lips against my mouth!

Strange and absurd that she could not banish the thought of Nicholas Brendon.

And then two amazing things happened unexpectedly and suddenly, as things sometimes do happen in life, when one least expects them. Toni had gone to bed the night before, dissatisfied and hopeless. She woke up to find a miracle had happened.

The miracle was a letter. An exhilarating letter to tell her that she had been left a thousand pounds by her godfather, an old man who had just died in a London nursing-home. It was a fortune for a girl who had had nothing.

Toni woke Helena up, shaking her violently.

'Helena! Wake! You must. You *must* listen. My dear, it's too marvellous!'

Yawning, Helena looked at her friend.

'What on earth has happened?'

14

'I've been left a legacy!'

Helena was wide awake at once.

'You lucky little beast! How much? Who from?'

'My old godfather. You know, I used to go and sit with him.'

'H'm! I'd go and sit at an old man's bedside for a month if I saw a cheque for five hundred quid coming to me.'

'Well, I didn't see it coming,' said Toni. 'It's simply wonderful, but I don't know what I'm going to do with all the money. What shall I do with it, Helena?'

'That's typical of you. My God! I'd know what to do with it, if it were mine. I could do with half of it. And you get a legacy! You, who tell me every damn night that love means more than money. It makes me sick!'

Instinctively, Toni's eyes sped to the mantelpiece and Nick's photograph.

Helena followed her gaze. She gave a hard little laugh.

'And I've had another letter from my dear Nick,' she added. 'It was waiting for me when I got in last night, posted by an optimist. He refuses to wait any longer. His partner has decided to stay in Canada and has deleted the marriage clause in the contract. Nick says he is doing quite well and enclosed the fare for the journey. He expects me to go to Cap Martin next week.'

Toni stared at Helena. Her legacy was

forgotten. She said with a little gasp:

'Oh, Helena! Do you mean it? He's really sent for you at last? You're going out to him *next* week?'

With a vicious gesture, Helena flung a thin sheet of notepaper across the bed to Toni.

'You can see for yourself what he says. But I'm not going! I'm *not*! I refuse to lead a rotten lonely life with a lot of smelling silver-foxes, just for the sake of making life more pleasant for Nick. I'd rather wear one round my neck and stay here with Bobby.'

Toni glanced at Nicholas Brendon's letter. One paragraph stood out:

I know you'll come, Helena my sweet. I'm intoxicated by the thought that you'll be here, sharing this house with me in a few days' time! Helena, when I close my eyes, I can feel you in my arms and it's almost intolerable ecstacy. Does so much love frighten you? Oh, my dear, I'll be very good to you . . .

Toni could read no more. A mist seemed to blot out the rest of the words. She trembled. This passion—this ardent desire of Nicholas Brendon for Helena—never failed to move, to excite her. She felt that it would be a crime for Helena to let him down, to disappoint him now at the eleventh hour.

'Helena!' she exclaimed. 'You can't refuse

16

to go out to Cap Martin now.'

'Oh yes, I can. And I will.'

'It would be too cruel. Nick adores you. Don't you care a rap for him any more?'

'Oh, I may regret losing his thrilling blue eyes and all that tosh,' Helena said, her eyes hardening. 'But I refuse to allow sentiment to overrule common sense. I need a rich man—all that Bobby can give me. No, Toni, I shall not go out to Nick, I shall break my engagement.'

'But you've led him on, all these months,' Toni argued. 'And you've said so often that he's a man well worth having. You told me he used to fool around with women but that he gave it all up for love of you. If you fail him now you'll do more than break his heart. You'll kill something fine in the man's very soul.'

Helena sprang to her feet.

'Bravo! What a grand speech, honey! You seem to have idealized old Nick. You're pleading his cause so brilliantly—I wonder you don't go out to Cap Martin in my place.'

Toni stared, then laughed.

'Don't be a fool, Helena.'

'But I'm serious!' Helena's dark eyes flashed. She looked at the cheque in Toni's hand. 'You don't want all that money. You haven't extravagant tastes like mine. And you've always said you envied me Nick. Very well. Take him. And give me the money. There you are! I'll *sell* him to you. Sell him for half

17

that cheque!' She broke off with a hysterical laugh.

Toni stared at her. She felt cold and then hot.

'You're quite mad, Helena.'

'No, I mean it. I want Bobby Deane. Five hundred pounds will give me the clothes and the cash to get him with. I'll write a letter to Nick, breaking my engagement. You can give it to him when you get there—pretend you've gone out for some other purpose. Most men fall for you, my dear. You're so pretty and charming. Nick adores your type. I can't think why he ever cared for me. He'll soon forget me and fall madly in love with you. You've only got to work things cleverly enough.'

Toni looked horrified.

'I'll do nothing of the sort. I've never heard of anything so outrageous.'

'All right,' said Helena. 'But I shan't change my mind. I shall write to Nick now that our engagement is off.'

'No, no, wait—' said Toni.

Somehow her eyes were drawn as though by a magnet to the photograph on the mantelpiece. Nick Brendon's handsome eyes smiled at her—lured her. The photograph, the whole personality of the man had always had a hypnotic effect on her. She felt that she was a little crazy, yet she could not help herself. And she could not tolerate the thought of Nick's agony of disappointment. Just a cold, cruel

18

telegram—then loneliness, an utter blank for him. She did not flatter herself that he would turn immediately to her for comfort, if she went out there. Yet she knew she could help. Any attractive woman could help to make things easier if she set herself out so to do. He would pour out his troubles—his heart. He might indeed turn to her on the rebound.

She had always envied Helena this lover of hers. And now she was being offered the chance to go to him. A mad scheme. Yet why not do it? If nothing more, it would be something for her to know that she had softened the blow for him.

Helena eyed her eagerly.

'Why don't you do it, Toni?' she said. 'Give me five hundred and go in my place next week. It will be an adventure. A marvellous thrill for you and I'm positive Nick will turn to you when you meet.'

Toni felt a strange shiver run through her body. She pressed her hands to her eyes. Already she seemed to feel Nick Brendon's arms about her and his voice saying: *'Help me, help me to forget.'*

It seemed a ludicrous and horrifying thing to purchase another girl's lover—a thing she would never have believed herself capable of doing. But she was tempted—and for Toni, temptation had lain in the lips, the eyes, the letters of Nicholas Brendon for so long.

She opened her eyes and looked at Helena

19

a trifle dazedly.

'If you really mean it,' she said, 'I'll do as you ask. I'll give you five hundred pounds and go out to Cap Martin in your place.'

CHAPTER TWO

The next few days seemed to Toni like a strange dream from which she must inevitably awake. A period of tense, throbbing excitement.

First, the purchase of suitable clothes. Then farewell to the old life, to Helena, who was delighted with her share of the bargain and certain of landing her 'fish'.

All the thrill and bustle of the boat-train platform at Victoria, the Channel crossing and the journey to Paris, where she had three hours to spend before she caught the night express down to the South. A new world was opening before her enchanted eyes. A new and exciting world in which was ever present the unfading vision of the man who waited for his future wife.

If she had any misgivings, any feelings of shame or disgust at the thing she was doing, Toni eliminated them by telling herself that it would have been worse for Nicholas Brendon if she hadn't made this decision. Helena would have broken with him anyhow—plunged him into gloom and disappointment and left him to bear it alone.

The hot Riviera sun was streaming into her sleeping-car when Toni opened her eyes that morning, after leaving England. She looked out of the window and found that the train was now passing through country of incredible beauty. Each station at which they stopped had a name which gave Toni a new thrill—*Cannes, Juan-les-Pins, Nice, Monte Carlo*!

At Monte Carlo, Toni began to collect her luggage and give her nose a final dab of powder: The next station would be Mentone. Nicholas would be waiting there.

At length the train steamed slowly into Mentone station, and Toni called for a porter.

She was pleased with her appearance. She looked cool and lovely in her new white clothes which she had put on that morning. But she felt chaotic inwardly. Her heart was pounding when at length she stood on the platform and looked for Nicholas Brendon. She had a swift confused vision of the glittering blue Mediterranean; palm trees, feathery green against the dazzling whiteness of the houses; gay gendarmes; porters in their blue blouses with dark, grinning faces. The platform was a mass of excited men and women searching for luggage and welcoming friends.

Then one figure stood out from all the rest and Toni saw no other.

She could not fail to recognize Nicholas Brendon, He was so exactly like his photograph. The tall, well-knit figure and the handsome dark head under the light felt hat which shielded him from the sun. Her heart gave a wild leap as she saw him searching the crowd on the platform—searching for Helena. She felt sick with pity for him, and mixed with that was a strange pity for herself because she was not the woman for whom he looked.

A moment later she had walked down the platform and stood before him.

'You are Mr. Brendon?' she asked.

'I am, yes. But I don't think I know . . .'

'No, of course not.' Toni coloured. She drew a letter from her bag. 'I am a friend of Miss Lane's. I have brought you a letter from her.'

She saw the eager light in his eyes die out. An expression of dismay came over his face.

'A message from Helena! But isn't she here—hasn't she come?'

'No, she isn't here. I'm most frightfully sorry. I'm afraid I've brought you very bad news.'

Nicholas Brendon stared at Toni.

'Bad news! Is she ill? Tell me quickly.'

'No, not ill,' said Toni. Then added the lie that Helena had prompted her to tell: 'As a matter of fact. Helena asked me to say that she can't come. She's never coming. She—oh well—she's married somebody else.'

For an instant a look of bewilderment screwed up Nicholas Brendon's face. Then the pain, the shock of the thing seemed to harden him. An expressionless mask came over his face. All tenderness was wiped off as though by a sponge. Even his voice changed; it became sarcastic and cold.

'So Helena sent you out here to tell me this? But why? A telegram would have done.'

Toni's cheeks were scarlet now.

'It's like this,' she stammered. 'I didn't come out specially to break this news. I was coming anyhow. Out to a job. So I brought Helena's letter with me. Here it is.'

Nicholas Brendon took the note and read it. Just a few terse words, typical of Helena.

Forgive me and forget me, Nick. We would never have got on and Bobby Deane is the right man for me. My friend, Toni Kenyon, is going to the Riviera, so I've asked her to break the news to you.

Good-bye,
Helena

Nicholas read the note through twice, then crushed it in his hand and put it in his pocket. Toni noticed that his were fine, brown, sensitive hands, not quite steady at the moment. This thing must be a bitter blow to Nicholas Brendon. Sensitive herself, she could see that the man's whole equilibrium was badly jarred. She admired his control. He said quietly:

'Thank you. So that's that! I'm sorry we haven't met under more amusing circumstances.'

Toni forgot that she had bargained with Helena for the purchase of this man. She remembered only that she had cared for him in a strange way long before she met him. Now that he stood before her, she thought that he was even more attractive than his photograph had suggested. His eyes were as blue as the sea, between thick dark lashes, and he had a smooth black head, and skin tanned to a deep bronze. At the moment, the handsome face was a mask. His lips were a thin hard line of pain. She wanted to break through that mask and comfort him for his own sake. She said impulsively:

'Oh—I'm so terribly sorry—but Helena didn't mean to hurt you so—please try to understand and forgive her . . .' Then, aware that what she said must sound ridiculous, she broke off and stood there helplessly.

Nicholas Brendan had forgotten her. He was lost—shaken to the depths of his soul by the blow Helena had dealt him. He had worked himself up to a pitch of nerves and excitement, waiting for her to arrive. He had spent hours rearranging his house—buying little things that he knew she would like. He had wanted her more than anything on earth.

And he had forgotten her faults.

During the year of their separation he had idealized her. Her letters had always been charming, if less passionate than his own. It was almost unendurable to find that she had not come—to know that she would never come; that he must go back and face that awful loneliness on his farm without hope—without promise. Heavens! It couldn't be true.

Toni said:

'We can't very well stand here like this, can we?'

He pulled himself together and tried to answer as though he were interested.

'Where do you wish to go, Miss—er—Kenyon?'

She hesitated.

She had decided to tell this man a lie. To say that she had neen coming out here as companion to an elderly lady but that the job had fallen through. A wire had reached her at Marseilles. She had come on to Mentone—especially to deliver Helena's message to him in person.

She hated telling that lie. Half hated herself for the bargain she had struck with Helena. Now that she saw Nicholas Brendon, she knew that she could love him utterly, completely. She would loathe him to know that she had 'bought' the right to come to Cap Martin in Helena's place. It was a place she might never be able to fill. She would, in all probability never be given the chance. Hadn't she been a little fool to come? Supposing Nicholas turned on his heel with a brief 'good-bye' and left her? Serve her right! It was what she deserved. Yet she felt slightly sick at the mere thought of losing him—just when she had found him. This one man in the world for her!

'Where are you going?' he asked her again.

She had to answer. She stammered her lie, without looking at the man. He believed it. Why not? He said:

'You mean that the woman has let you down, now you're out here?'

'Yes,' said Toni. 'She had other plans.'

'A bit tricky to land a girl here with nowhere to go and nothing to do,' said Nicholas. 'With all due respect to your sex, some women appear to have no scruples.'

Toni felt guilty, but she said no more. Nicholas Brendon's blue eyes rested for an instant on the scarlet flower of her mouth. For the first time he saw her clearly.

'Lord, how pretty the child is,' he thought. 'Can't be more than twenty or so. Younger than Helena. But I wonder if she's any more trustworthy. I don't think I shall ever trust a woman again.'

'We seem to be in the same trouble. Each given the slip. Look here, you can't stay alone here. The Riviera isn't the place for a young, unattached girl as pretty as you are.'

Toni's blood stirred. She so wanted him to

26

think her pretty. But she still had that sense of guilt—the feeling that he would despise her—that he would not want to be kind to her if he knew that transaction between Helena and herself. For some absurd reason the tears came into her eyes. He saw them.

'But you're crying,' he said. 'Why? My dear child, you can't be crying for me! Please! What do I matter? You ask me to understand and forgive Helena. I'll forgive gladly. But I can't understand—how can I? I thought she cared for me.'

Toni looked away from him. Her face was as pale now as it had been red.

'I'm so terribly sorry,' she repeated.

'You needn't be,' he said and laughed suddenly, hardly. 'I'm not going to break my heart over Helena. The world is full of beautiful women—there are thousands of them. Surely I'm talking now to the prettiest girl who has ever set foot in France!'

He laughed again. But his mouth was hard as steel. Toni was infinitely compassionate. Who could blame him if the devil that was in him—and perhaps there was more of the devil in Nicholas Brendon than in most men—broke through the mask of pain and chuckled a bit? He had loved Helena so faithfully, so tenderly. His love had been thrown back in his face.

'I wish I knew what to say,' she whispered.

'Come and talk to me. We'll drive down to the Casino and have a drink together.'

Later, they sat on the terrace of the Casino, facing the incredible blue of the sea. She was drinking a tomato-juice cocktail. He, with a gin-fizz in one hand and a cigarette in the other, questioned her about the future.

'Can't this woman take you to live with her for a bit, until you get another job? . . . She can't—then you'll have to go back to England.'

Toni gave him a nervous look.

'I don't want to go back to England.'

He laughed, his eyes roving restlessly over the crowds on the gay terrace.

'Mediterranean madness!' he said. 'It's got you already.'

'It's not madness,' she said, sipping her drink. 'I've always wanted to see the Riviera. Why should I turn tail now and run home to England? I think *that* would be madness. I've got a little ready money and I'm sure to find another job. I might even break the bank at Monte Carlo!'

Nicholas threw away his cigarette.

'You won't break the bank,' he said slowly. 'And you'll find it difficult to get a job. I'm afraid you're up against it. We both are. You lose a job and I lose a wife. I'd arranged to celebrate with Helena this afternoon. Well, instead I shall get tight in the club.'

She shook her head gravely at him.

'That won't do you much good. You will merely get morbid and have a hang-over to add to your troubles in the morning.'

28

He liked the easy, friendly way she said that. He shrugged his shoulders and grinned at her like a schoolboy. But she could see that his nerves were at breaking-point. He was making a poor attempt at hiding the disappointment and disillusionment which he felt.

'My dear child, the hang-over would be worth it if I could really drown my sorrows in drink,' he said.

'But you know you can't. And there's always tomorrow.'

'To hell with tomorrow!' Nicholas raised his glass. 'But perhaps you're right. Drink is not the only consolation. I can find some dazzling blonde and take her out and make love to her. We might drive through the pinewoods and watch the moon over the sea. I'll tell her how jealous I am of the moonlight because it kisses her cheeks. And in the morning I'll write a note to say that I'm sorry that it wasn't the moonlight after all, but the reflection from the flood-lit Casino at Monte.'

As he stopped speaking, Toni put a hand on his arm.

'Poor, poor you! I know how you must feel.'

Nicholas turned towards her and saw that there were tears in her eyes. He felt guilty and embarrassed. He was a swine to burden her with his sorrows. He had always loved women and respected them until he received this last blow from Helena. There was no reason to make her friend miserable. Toni had obviously loathed the task of breaking the news to him.

'Listen,' he said, 'for heaven's sake don't cry. It's not worth it. I'll get over it and anyhow why should you upset yourself over my troubles?'

'I don't know,' she said, 'except, as I say, I am so sorry about it all.'

'It's decent of you to feel like that,' he said. 'I'm sorry you had to be bothered with the affair. Did you know Helena well?'

'Yes. She lived with me.'

Nicholas looked at her with sudden interest. So this was the girl whose flat Helena had shared. Toni Kenyon! He remembered the name now. Helena had told him that the flat in Earls Court was owned by a girl who worked with her. An attractive little thing, Helena had described her once, he remembered. She had suggested that he would admire her type.

'So Helena lived with you,' Nicholas repeated. 'In that case you can probably tell me why she changed her mind. Is she really in love with this fellow—what do you call him?'

'Bobby Deane,' Toni said. 'Well, I think Helena probably does love him in her own way. She says that he has everything which she needs to make her happy—both money and position.'

'Has she known him long?'

'He arrived a few months ago—in a marvellous Rolls-Bentley. He took her out to Ranelagh to see his polo ponies, and all over the place. I believe he fell in love with her at first sight.'

Nicholas threw away his cigarette and shaded his eyes from the glare of the sun.

'And you think,' he asked, looking at Toni, 'that she loves the man—not the Bentley and the polo ponies?'

'I think so, but perhaps if you'd been on the spot things might have been different. You must remember that when Helena first met Bobby, she thought there was little chance of marrying you for at least another year.'

'I think you're being very loyal to her,' said Nicholas with a touch of sarcasm in his voice, 'but just tell me this. When you last saw Helena, had she heard about my legacy?'

'Legacy!' Toni repeated. 'No, I don't think so. She never mentioned it.'

'I thought not,' Nicholas gave a short laugh. 'You see I'm quite a wealthy man now. My partner died and left me the farm and his money. I wrote the news to Helena. The letter must have arrived just after you left.'

Toni put out a hand and touched his arm.

'I'm so glad he left you the money,' she said impulsively. 'I know how you've had to slave at your work out here. Things will be easier for you now. God knows you deserve a bit of luck!'

Nicholas smiled.

'It's very kind of you. Things will certainly be easier although I shan't be able to afford polo-ponies just yet!'

'You don't need polo-ponies in order to be happy,' Toni answered. 'Anyhow, I'm sure I should prefer silver foxes!'

Nicholas was moved by this girl's frankness and sympathy. He had to admit that she appeared to be a grand kid. Why should she cry for him? She had never seen him before in her life. He didn't suppose she had ever heard of him more than casually from Helena.

A sudden thought flashed through his mind.

'Look here,' he said. 'You've been disappointed today—let down by this woman who brought you out. You don't want to go back to England. You say you have no ties and that you need a job. Shall I offer you one?'

Toni caught her breath. There could be no doubt that Nicholas appeared interested in her.

'What sort of a job can you offer me?' she smiled.

'A job as my housekeeper,' he said, crossing his legs and taking another cigarette from the thin gold case. 'I've only a lot of lazy servants on my farm. The house needs a woman's management. I've fixed up such a pretty bedroom for my wife. It seems a pity to waste it. Let me offer it to you. Why don't you come on a month's trial—shall we say at a salary to be agreed upon?'

'But what about a chaperone?' Toni asked. 'It's a bit difficult to plant oneself in a bachelor's house where there isn't another woman.'

Nicholas nodded.

'Quite right! But there's Marie, my old French cook. She would probably mother you.'

'I don't want to be "mothered". I'm thinking of your reputation more than my own. I don't know anyone out here. I've no one in the world to bother about what I do. But all your friends, what will they think of you?'

'The worst, I imagine,' Nicholas answered with a grin. 'It will be round the clubs in a couple of days. Not that I give a damn. It's entirely up to you.'

Toni was silent for a moment. She felt a thrill of excitement run through her body. She had won! Things were working out just as Helena had predicted. Nicholas was turning to her on the rebound. He wanted her for his housekeeper. That was an absurd job, of course, made especially for her. He had asked her for a whim—out of his own loneliness—perhaps. Perhaps even out of pity for her. Well, she knew that there was nothing she would like to do more than to follow him to the ends of the earth.

She looked up at him with wide-open serious eyes.

'You are really being serious?' she asked.

Nicholas Brendon rose and gave a musical comedy bow. His expression was cynical but not unfriendly as he spoke.

'My house and I are at your disposal. But I

warn you—I may not be your idea of a charming employer. This thing Helena has done to me has stripped me of any tender illusions I may have had about women. I shall never trust a woman again. And I don't ask you to trust me. We shall be alone on a very lonely farm. Are you scared?'

If Toni felt uneasy she did not show it. She looked him squarely in the eyes and said:

'No. I'm not afraid of anything.'

'Not even of a disappointed man who is used to taking what he wants and to having his wishes granted?'

The rich, insolent voice made her wince but she continued to meet his gaze.

'I think you're dramatizing yourself.'

'Not in the least. Believe me, I've been a plaster saint for Helena's sake. Now I'm going to go places and do things.'

'What difference should that make to me—where you go and what you do when you get there?'

His eyes narrowed and rested on the red curve of her mouth.

'It might make a lot of difference to you—what I do at Cap Martin.'

The battle of words intrigued and excited her. She said suddenly:

'Mr. Brendon—I'm not a fool—but tell me one thing, are you asking me to be your housekeeper or your "girlfriend"?'

The words seemed to bring Nicholas back

34

to earth with a jolt. The devil in him took a back seat. The sinister look in his eyes faded back to normal.

'My dear child,' he said, putting his hand on her arm, 'of course, I'm asking you to come as my housekeeper. I just want to show you that I'm not the synthetic saint which Helena may have painted me. You can rely on me—if you'll come. But why not leave me to get out of this mess in my own particular way? Why don't you run home to England?'

For an instant she did not reply. She realized that it was a wild step to take—to accept this job as housekeeper to a man whom she had only met an hour ago. Nicholas had warned her that he might be a difficult employer to deal with. But she knew that she never wanted to leave him again; that saint or no saint he was, in a curious way, deep in the heart of her. She said quietly:

'I want to accept your offer.'

'You will? And risk a scandal that will ring through the English colony here?'

'Yes.'

'You're plucky,' Nicholas said, 'or a little fool. I'm not sure which. Let's go!'

He drained his glass. Over the rim he smiled at Toni. Fate offered him this golden-eyed girl with the primrose hair; offered him her companionship to make life on his farm a little less boring and lonely. He would be a fool to turn down such a gift of the gods. At this

35

moment he should have been in the Mentone registrar's office with Helena. Perhaps the gods believed in the law of compensation!

CHAPTER THREE

A week later, Toni stood on the verandah of Nick Brendon's house. She shaded her eyes from the glare of the sun and looked down the hill over the farm; over lonely, aching miles of dusty, sun-burnt trees almost grey-green against the hard blue of the sky. In the distance she could see the gaily coloured sails of the fishing boats on the sea.

She was waiting for Nick to come home.

Every day, like this, just before sundown, she waited. All through the hot, solitary hours while he worked on the farm she did what she could to make the time pass. There was little for her to do except encourage the servants in the house to work; dust or mend; try to make life more comfortable than usual for Nick.

On the first day of her arrival Toni had found the cook, Marie, a little difficult. The old French woman was truculent and obviously jealous of the lovely young English girl whom her beloved Monsieur Brendon had brought to the house. Toni went out of her way to win Marie's affection and regard. If she continued to be hostile she could, Toni realized, make

36

life complicated. But by the end of the week Marie had become the young housekeeper's friend and ally. They found that they had a common bond—Nick Brendon—and they agreed to pull together in order to make things as pleasant as possible for him.

At first the heat of the Riviera summer worried Toni. But it did not destroy her energy. She was never weary of performing those small domesticated jobs for the man to whom she was housekeeper. She only wished that she might be busier during the days.

It gave her immense satisfaction to mend his clothes; to see that he had the food he liked, to fill the place with beautifully arranged flowers. She knew that Helena had never been domesticated, and had always loathed sewing. It pleased her to think that she was doing more for Nick than Helena could have done. And he was grateful. Every night he told her that it made all the difference in the world to him to come back and see the woman's touch in the house; the flowers in the rooms; his drinks ready and iced; cigarette box full, and herself, 'the little housekeeper', fresh and cheerful, ready in an attractive frock to give him the feminine companionship for which he had always yearned.

'It was hell until you came, Toni,' he had told her yesterday.

She believed it. How lonely he must have been in spite of his partner. She, herself, found it incredibly lonely here. But she learned to like it and much more than that. For now she loved this man in all his moods. He was friendly, grateful, although sometimes the bitterness of disappointments, resentment against the woman who had thrown him over, made him callous and cynical. He was curt, even rude to Toni. Then she did not mind and he was amazed at her patience, her understanding of the devil that was in him.

On the first Sunday after she came to Cap Martin, he drove his big two-seater Packard from the garage round to the house, and sounded the horn.

Toni, wondering what the noise was about, put her head out of the bedroom window where she was working. She saw him looking up at her.

'Come along!' he called. 'We're going for a drive.'

Her eyes sparkled but she shook her head.

'My dear Nick, I haven't nearly finished my work. I haven't even ordered the meals.'

'Tell Marie we'll be out for food,' he shouted. 'Go and get your things on and don't argue with your boss!'

Toni was only too ready to submit to such an order. She ran to her bedroom and changed her clothes. This was heaven! She would spend the whole day with him. She would be at his side in the car. They would lunch and dine together; she would have him to herself until they returned at night.

She came out of the house to find Nick holding the car door open. He had never seen her looking more beautiful—slim and chic in a white, sleeveless dress and jade-green scarf; her complexion matching the peach-pink rose which she was wearing; her hair sleek, shining in the sun.

'You look sweet,' he said.

He took his place behind the wheel and steered the car down the drive. He felt that life was good. It was a perfect day with a cooling breeze from the sea which made driving a pleasure. The Packard went like a bird.

When they had breasted the hill above Mentone, Nicholas drew up and turned towards Toni.

'Choose your route,' he said, pointing to the road which wound along the coast below them. 'To the right, Monte Carlo, Nice, Cannes—sophisticated and artificial but very amusing. To the left Italy—Bordighera, San Remo and "blackshirts"!'

Toni chose Italy.

The car passed through the old Roman gate outside Mentone, then turned towards the frontier. It was an exciting, twisty road. On one side a row of orange-tiled villas, gardens flaming with roses, carnations and geraniums, and on the other always the eternal blue of the sea.

It was fun when they were held up at the

customs. A smiling officer searched the car and examined their passports. He was a handsome young man in a splendid uniform. When he closed the door of the car he saluted Toni with more than usual interest.

'These fellows like a pretty woman.' Nick laughed. 'I'd better keep my eye on you!'

All the men were smiling and they seemed to wear different uniforms. It reminded Toni of a Ruritanian musical comedy. She gave a little cry of delight when she saw the first 'blackshirt' and thrilled at the sight of a life-size photograph of Mussolini on the wall of a shop.

Nick usually drove the Packard at a high speed but today he handled it with care. He wanted to make the drive last as long as possible. He had a precious passenger in the car. Life was no longer a solitary responsibility. And he found it amusing to watch Toni's reactions. She was so thrilled by everything she saw. He could not have found a more appreciative companion.

They lunched at a little restaurant outside Bordighera. It was owned by a man named Benito. Nick swore he was the best restaurant manager who had ever left London. The cooking was superlative.

When they entered, Benito ran forward and bowed.

'This is indeed an honour, Signor, that you bring the Signora here so soon after your marriage.'

Toni felt her cheeks grow scarlet. Of course! The man had heard that Nick was to be married. He thought that she was Helena. She dreaded the effect that the little Italian's words would have upon Nick. She was soon put at her ease. Nick slapped his friend on the back and laughed.

'I'm not married, Benito, this is Miss Kenyon, my housekeeper. I've told her that you have the best food in Italy, so see what you can do.'

'You are very kind, Signor,' Benito beamed. 'I will attend to everything myself.'

Nick led Toni to a white terrace which was shaded from the heat of the sun by striped umbrellas. He insisted that she should drink a champagne-cocktail to celebrate their first holiday; that she should share a bottle of Chianti with him for lunch.

It was a perfect meal that Benito served them. Fresh trout from the tank in the kitchen, followed by a huge dish of tomatoes, green and red pimentoes, radishes, celery and lettuce. Later while they drank coffee Benito plucked a handful of warm, ripe figs from the tree which shaded the terrace and put them on their table.

Toni felt her spirits rise. Nick appeared to be untroubled by Benito's allusions to his marriage. She wondered if it were possible that the wound was beginning to heal, or if he just acted this way in order not to spoil her day. Certainly, she had never seen him in such good form. He was considerate, the perfect host; nothing was too good for her. What a fool Helena had been to throw him over! He could make any woman ideally happy.

After lunch they lay back in long wicker chairs until Nick, jumping to his feet, threw away the cigarette he was smoking.

'Come along,' he said, 'if we stay here we shall go to sleep. I've got lots to show you.'

They climbed into the Packard and turned towards San Remo. Toni gave herself up once again to the enjoyment of the drive. They kept to the old Roman road, through the little town of Ospedaletti from where they looked across the bay towards San Remo.

San Remo seemed to her a city of palms and flowers. Nick drove her through the old part of the town; up and down the vaulted streets and narrow alleys of the Middle Ages. Eventually they turned along the principal promenade and drew up outside the Casino.

'This is where I lose my new-found fortune,' Nick said, and led her towards the gambling rooms.

A Casino was quite strange and novel to Toni. She liked to watch the inscrutable faces of the croupiers as they raked in little piles of chips; the tense expressions of the smartly dressed crowd that gathered round the tables. Nick gave her a handful of the plaques which she threw on different numbers. The first time her number won she gave a little cry of excitement:

'Let's go now, Nick,' she said, 'if we stay we're sure to lose it all.'

He laughed.

'You are a baby. Put your money in your bag and we'll go and dance.'

There was an English dance-band in the ballroom. It had perfect rhythm which Toni, a born dancer, was quick to appreciate. Nick saw her beating out the time with her foot.

'You like dancing?' he asked.

'Love it.'

'So do I,' he said, rising to his feet, 'let's show these people how it's done.'

Toni found him the perfect partner. His most intricate steps were easy to follow. His whole body seemed to answer to the rhythm of the band and was one with hers. Sometimes he crooned a few lines of the better-known choruses in his low, husky voice. He had found the ideal partner and he told Toni so.

'We must practise at home,' he said. 'We'll probably turn out to be another Astaire–Rogers partnership.'

'I'm sure that Marie would not approve of a dancing housekeeper.'

He flung back his head and laughed.

'To blazes with Marie! Let's go and have a drink.'

The silver-and-green cocktail-bar was

crowded when they entered. The barman came forward and led them to one of the few remaining tables in a corner of the room. Nick ordered the drinks and glanced round the crowded tables.

'Do you know many people here?' Toni asked.

'A few. I see George Adams, one of my pet aversions. Good Heavens, he's coming over here!'

Toni disliked Adams on sight. He was a swarthy overdressed young man with a drawl. When Nick introduced them he took Toni's hand and touched it with his lips. It made her shudder. The man looked at her with clouded eyes. They reminded Toni of the eyes of a well-fed snake.

She finished her drink which the waiter had brought and rose to her feet.

'I must go and powder my nose. Thanks for the cocktail, Nick.'

Adams watched her slim figure cross the room.

'Who's the "girl-friend", Brendon?' he asked, turning towards Nick.

'My housekeeper, Miss Kenyon. Didn't you hear her name when I introduced you?'

Adams gave a short laugh.

'Housekeeper! You're a cunning old devil! But I admit I admire your taste. She's a winner. You must give me the address of the domestic agency where you got her.'

Nick felt the blood rush to his face.

'Shut up, Adams. Just because you happen to have a foul mind there's no need to—'

'Don't ride the high horse, old man,' Adams interrupted, 'I don't care how you amuse yourself on your farm. I'd do the same if I was in your position. That's what I said in the club the other night when they were discussing your new friend.'

Nick jumped to his feet.

'Listen, Adams. I'd be glad if you and your cheap pals would refrain from discussing me.'

He turned on his heel and walked across the room. They were a rotten set these wealthy playboys who infested the Riviera, he thought. And they had been talking about him already. Well, they had a good story for once!

Toni met him at the door of the bar. She wondered why he looked so flushed, if he was feeling ill.

'Is anything the matter?' she asked quickly.

Nick lit a cigarette.

'I've got a headache, a touch of sun probably. Do you mind if we go?'

Toni did not enjoy the drive home. Nick was silent. No longer was he the gay, charming companion of that golden day. He was in one of the moods which she learned to dread; when he appeared to resent her existence.

He drove the Packard as if pursued by a pack of devils who were determined to crush him. He was thinking how happy he had been

45

today. He had forgotten Helena. Toni Kenyon, who had come so suddenly, so strangely into his life, had blotted out the pain, the disappointment. He had found her an ideal companion both in and out of the house. He knew quite well that she made all the difference to his life. But it was not until the George Adams incident that he realized that he was falling in love with her.

He dreaded lest she might leave him. In a vague way he also dreaded the fact that he loved her. She was sweet and charming. But could he believe her? He knew little about her. Less than he had known about Helena when they became engaged. And he had vowed never to love another woman; never to trust another. He was probably a weak-kneed fool to fall for the next pretty face which came his way. He must try to get a grip on himself; dismiss her from his mind. It would hurt her, he knew, if he was cool and off-hand. But it would give him a fierce sadistic satisfaction because he, himself, had been so hurt.

He had drunk more than usual. He carried a whisky into the drawing-room—the white-and-blue room which he had made beautiful for Helena. He lounged there in an easy chair and smoked. He scarcely raised his eyes to Toni. Yet she was looking her best tonight, in a black net dinner-frock which she had brought out with her.

It was a sweltering night; not a breath of air

indoors or out. Toni felt languid and deeply depressed. She attempted to liven the atmosphere by putting a record on the gramophone. A man was singing:

'I've got a woman crazy for me,
She's funny that way.
Why should I leave her, why should I go
She'd be unhappy without me, I know.
I'm only human and a coward at best
I'm certain that woman would follow me West!'

Nick stirred in his chair and put his pipe in his pocket.

'For God's sake turn that thing off. It's as old as the hills.'

'Sorry,' she said, turning off the machine. 'It's a favourite of mine.'

Nick stood up and walked to the door that opened on to the verandah. His tall white-clad figure was silhouetted against the dark sky.

'It's a damned silly song. "Unhappy without me"! The fellow who's singing it has been divorced three times.'

'You're in a rotten mood, Nick. You'll probably be singing it yourself, tomorrow.'

'If there was a woman crazy for me I wouldn't sing at all. The experience is too nerve-racking.'

Toni said nothing. Tonight she was blind to the reason for this almost savage mood.

47

He turned and gave her a queer, sulky look.

'Listen, Toni,' he added. 'That fellow, Adams, told me that we are being discussed at the Club. They don't swallow the "housekeeper" story. You can't expect them to. Hadn't you better pack up and go?'

She felt the blood drain from her face.

'If you think it best,' he said.

He looked at her; the lovely, youthful figure in the frilly gossamer dress; the fair hair touched to gold by the lamplight; the wistful, beautiful face. If he 'thought it best'! God knows, he didn't want her to go. It was impossible to imagine life without her. But Helena had hurt him so. He didn't want to risk being hurt again—by any woman. Yet he believed he could live happily with Toni. She was different from Helena—generous and unsophisticated. She had proved it since she had come to Cap Martin. She had worked for him without real reward or many thanks.

He said:

'I do think it's best. I'll try to find another job for you—that is if you want to stay in the South of France.'

'But, Nick, you said you wouldn't mind the gossip,' she said. 'Don't you remember you told me you didn't in the least care about what the people here said?'

Nick nodded and turned towards the door.

'I remember. But I've changed my mind. Things haven't worked out as I expected. I'm going out now—you'd better decide where you want to go.'

After he had gone, Toni sat down in a chair. She felt crushed and disappointed. Nick didn't seem to care whether she went today or tomorrow. He was cold and ruthless. And she had thought she was quite settled in the house; that he was happy with her. Probably it was too much to ask; that she should be allowed to stay with the man for whom she had gambled with Helena. The gods had a nasty way of tripping one up when things appeared just right. They were probably sharing the joke with Nick's devil.

A low growl of thunder disturbed the silence of the night. Toni shivered. She hated thunderstorms; the violent sort of storms that broke over the Riviera. Nick had gone out, left her, probably driven down to the town to drink with that hopeless crowd in the Club. He would tell them that she was leaving; that their latest bit of scandal had come to an end.

The storm broke with sudden, smashing violence over the farm. A loud clap of thunder echoed across the hills; the room was illuminated by a vivid streak of lightning.

Toni sprang up with a cry.

It was raining now, a heavy soaking rain which beat against the window-panes. The thunder sounded like a battery of howitzers in action. Fork-lightning played wickedly across the surcharged heavens.

For a moment she watched, breathlessly, a huge gaily coloured moth, fluttering over the oil-lamp on the table. It suddenly dropped down the tall old-fashioned globe and extinguished the light. Another vivid flash of lightning lit up the darkened room.

Toni stumbled towards the door.

'Nick,' she cried. 'Nick, where are you?'

The next moment the wire-door swung open. Nick came in, white suit drenched, black hair plastered against his head. He was smiling.

'What a beauty! That last flash lit up the whole of Mentone. What the devil's happened to the light. Toni . . .'

She stood still, unable to speak.

The next flash of lightning lit up her face. He saw that she was crying.

'Toni!'

He walked towards her, hands outstretched, groping. Then his hands found her, rested on her slim bare arms as he pulled her towards him. He felt the warmth of her slim, young body against his.

'What's the matter, my dear? Are you all right?'

'The storm,' she said. 'It frightened me. I thought you'd gone. I'm a fool but—'

He put a hand against her mouth.

'Ssh! I'm the fool, darling. I shouldn't have left you. I know I can never leave you again, never!'

She was in his arms, sobbing with relief.

'It wasn't only the storm which frightened me. Oh, Nick! I love you—don't send me away. I should die.'

He held her fiercely. The restraint of the last days was forgotten. He was a man in love, with this woman in his arms. He buried his face against her neck.

'I can never leave you,' he repeated.

Toni felt her body tremble in his arms. She did not think. They stood together oblivious of everything except the realization that they had found each other. The misery, the doubt, the despair of the last days were swept away.

He put a hand beneath her chin and tilted the fair head backwards.

'Kiss me!'

The storm raged on, shaking the house. The thunder crashed and echoed from the hills. The rain came down in a vast stream of water.

After a long silence, Nick raised his head and covered her face with kisses.

'I love you, Toni. You know I love you?'

'Yes,' she whispered. 'And I love you.'

'It's more than I deserve. I've been a brute—a moody, ungrateful swine.'

'I've understood.'

'You've been grand to me, Toni. I was foul because I felt myself falling in love with you. I didn't want to. After the débâcle with Helena I wanted to keep love out of my life. But if I wanted that, I shouldn't have brought you

51

here.'

'Darling, darling, Nick,' she cried. 'You must never be hurt again. I love you so terribly, with all my heart and soul. I want nothing else on earth but you—you!'

He held her closer, as if frightened that she would escape.

'Then tomorrow you must marry me and come back here as my wife. I shall be an intolerable husband. I shall never let you out of my sight. I shall lock all the doors and keep you veiled. It's hardly fair to a man to have such a beautiful wife!'

She did not know whether she was crying or laughing.

'Do you love me as much as you loved Helena?'

Nick laughed.

'I'm glad you asked that question. It's so utterly feminine. The answer is easy. I'm grateful to her for having sent you here with that letter; for having brought real love into my life. It's the best thing she ever did for me.'

'Darling Nick!'

Suddenly he picked her up in his arms.

'Now it's late, darling, you must go to bed, but before you go, tell me once again that you love me.'

She answered with utter conviction.

'I shall always love you.'

He carried her upstairs and laid her on her bed. She put out a hand which he crushed to his lips.

'Sleep well, lovely, kind little Toni. You've shown me a one-way road to paradise,' he whispered. 'Tonight I say good night to my little housekeeper; tomorrow I shall say good night to my wife.'

Long after he had left her, Toni was awake, staring into the darkness. It was impossible to sleep. She had so many thoughts of tomorrow, when she would be the wife of the one man whom she had always loved. Yes, she had loved him since she had first seen that photograph of him and heard what Helena had to say. Then she remembered that she had bought him from Helena; that she had gambled for Nick, for his love. The cards had turned in her favour; she had won the game. But she had cheated. She sent up an impassioned appeal to the gods to spare him from ever knowing the truth. For his sake so much more than her own.

CHAPTER FOUR

Nicholas Brendon's Packard climbed the long dusty hill leading up from the registrar's office in Mentone where he had just married Toni Kenyon, and turned into the garden of his house.

Beside him sat Toni, her hand clasped

tightly in his. She was dumb with happiness. She looked a mere child in her white dress with the big white hat on her fair head. Her eyes glowed at him under their dark lashes; her cheeks seemed to be one warm blush of happiness.

Nick felt like a boy out of school. He told Toni so.

'I can't believe it, darling,' he said. 'I just can't believe that you're my wife. That you will be with me for the rest of my life.'

She put his hand against her cheek.

'But it's true, darling Nicky.'

'Love me?'

'Terribly.'

'Never terribly enough.'

The car drew up outside the house. Nicholas bent to kiss her. Toni put a finger to his lips.

'The servants!' she laughed. 'They're watching us from every window in the house.'

'To blazes with the servants. You're enough to make any bridegroom mad.'

'I feel quite mad, myself.'

He jumped out of the car and opened the door for her. He insisted upon carrying her out of the car into the house.

'We're going to spend a few days here, darling,' he said, 'and then I'm going to take my wife to see the wonders of the world. I want to show you off to everybody. So far I just can't realize my good fortune.'

Toni closed her eyes as she lay in his arms. It was heaven to be here with him, in their own home. All she wanted was to stay with him, to make him happy.

He carried her through the hall towards the drawing-room which Marie had decorated with scarlet and purple flowers in honour of their marriage. Then he opened the door and she felt his grip suddenly tighten.

'Good God,' he said, *'Helena!'*

Toni opened her eyes. Her heart gave a violent jerk. She had a confused vision of the tall, dark girl who stood waiting for them in the flower-decked room.

Nick set Toni on her feet. Holding on to her hand, he stared across the room towards Helena. He said:

'What are you doing here?'

Helena came forward slowly.

'Nick, my dear, is that all you've got to say to me?'

'What are you doing here?'

Helena shot a lightning glance towards Toni who stood with her hand in Nick's.

'You—you two aren't . . . ?'

'Married? Yes, an hour ago. Aren't you going to congratulate us?' Nick asked in an icy voice.

Helena's dark eyes flashed dangerously. She felt sick with disappointment. She was too late. An hour too late. Toni had landed her fish, married him.

It was a blow to Helena. The second blow to her vanity, to her ambitions within the last few days. She had received Nick's letter telling of his sudden prosperity on the day Toni left England. It did not worry her. She counted on Bobby Deane's millions. But Bobby let her down with a jerk which had more than wounded her pride. At the first suggestion of marriage, he had disappeared into the night in his Bentley. She had not seen him again. When she realized that he was gone for good, Helena packed her bags and came to Mentone with all possible speed. She was determined to marry Nick. She believed that if she could get there in time it would be easy to lie her way out of her previous actions.

She gave a gesture of despair and turned towards Nick.

'So I'm just an hour too late to save you.'

'To save me from what?' he asked coldly.

'From your sweet little baby-bride,' she said with an hysterical laugh. 'She seems to have found you easy game. I thought you were too old, Nick, to be caught by a head of golden curls and a "hard-luck" story!'

Toni gasped. What was Helena going to tell him about her? What did she intend to do? She soon knew. Helena paced the room pouring out her story. She spoke convincingly, with the skill of the born liar.

Toni had shared the flat in Cromwell Road with her; had proved herself to be a liar and a cheat. She, Helena, had been the fool. She had befriended Toni, because she felt sorry for her. She had confided her most intimate secrets to the girl in the belief that she was a real friend. How wrong she had been! She had told Toni that she was expecting to go out to Mentone to marry Nick; that he was sending the money for the tickets. It was obvious that Toni had intercepted the letter. Helena had waited in vain for three long weeks, she said, for the tickets and for news. She had received neither so she had borrowed the money and rushed to Mentone.

'I've been mad with misery, Nick, darling,' she finished, with tears streaming down her face.

Nicholas Brendon stared at Helena in horror. He had dropped Toni's hand. The colour had drained from his face.

'You mean you didn't break off our engagement, in order to marry Deane?'

'Of course not. I've never been unfaithful to you for a single moment.'

'But you wrote me a letter—the letter Toni brought.'

Helena gave a short laugh.

'My *dear* Nick, I never wrote that letter. The letter Toni brought! You know I always type my letters to you. Toni used my typewriter. She knew my signature as well as her own. That was easy.'

'It's a lie,' Toni broke in. 'It isn't true.'

57

She went across to Helena and stood face to face with her.

'What have you done this for?'

'I've nothing to say to you.'

'Helena. You can't be so mean, so vile . . .'

She broke off. The look in Helena's face astounded her. It was so hard. It was impossible to believe that this girl who had been her friend and who had shared her life and virtually sold Nick, could be here now pretending to be injured and innocent.

'Helena, for your own sake tell Nick the truth.'

Deliberately Helena turned her back on Toni.

'I don't want to speak to you. What you've done to Nick and me is too vile for words.'

Nicholas put a hand on his wife's shoulder.

'Listen, Toni,' he said. 'We've got to get this straight. You've heard what Helena has said, now tell her your story. Tell her how you came out here to work for some elderly English woman. How you—'

'What!' Helena broke in, 'that's funny! Ask her the name—where she lived.'

'What was this woman's address, Toni?' Nick asked her.

'I can't remember.'

Nick gripped her arm.

'Don't be a fool, Toni. You must know her name, where she lived. Tell me quickly.'

Toni looked at him speechlessly. She felt

58

stupefied with fear. It was impossible to give him a logical explanation of her actions. No man would believe her story that she had *bought* him from Helena. It would be easy for him to prove that the woman who was to have employed her, had never existed. Then he would never trust her again. He would believe in Helena.

She tried to speak, to make some feeble excuse, but the words would not come. Suddenly she turned and ran towards her bedroom away from them—away from Nick's accusing eyes. He started to follow her but Helena stopped him.

'Wait a minute, Nick, I want to speak to you by yourself.'

He looked at her despairingly.

'There must be some mistake,' he said. 'I know Toni can explain things. It's all a mess. She is hysterical. She didn't know what she was saying just now. It was the surprise—finding you here.'

Helena put a hand on his arm.

'I feel terribly sorry for you, Nick. It's the very devil for you—for us both. Don't forget that I've always loved you, that I expected to come here as your wife.'

Nick stared at her. It was fantastic. Helena still loved him; she had been faithful to him; had come out to him. If her story was true, then he had married a crook. But that was impossible. There must be an explanation and he must find it out.

'Wait here, Helena,' he said. 'I'm going to see Toni now. One of you is lying to me and I intend to find out which.'

Helena made a gesture with her hand.

'As you like.'

Nicholas ran up the stairs and flung open the door of his wife's bedroom. Toni was sitting on the edge of the bed, her face covered with her hands.

'Tell me this isn't true, Toni,' he implored her. 'Tell me that Helena is lying—that you did come out to work for some woman. You know her name—you must know it. You must.'

Toni looked up at him in despair.

'That was a lie, Nick. The only lie I've told you. It's all a terrible mix-up. But you must believe me when I say that I love you—that I married you because I love you.'

His face was set and hard as he watched her.

'Then what Helena says is true. You came out here to find a husband, not a job. Do you deny that you opened my letter; that you used the ticket which I sent her?'

'I deny that. It isn't true.'

'Then how else did you know which day she was coming—when she was coming out to be married to me?'

'She told me—'

'And you slid into her shoes?'

'No—I—'

Her voice trailed away hopelessly. She was

60

shivering violently. She realized that she was cornered—that it would only make matters worse if she began to stammer out the story of her cheque and how she had given the money to Helena in exchange for that ticket which had brought her out here. He had every reason to think that she was a liar and a cheat.

'You have no explanation?' he asked, once again.

'Not one that I can make.'

'Then Helena is right. Good God, you admit she is right!'

'No, Nick. When she says that I tricked her, that I deliberately married you she lies, and she knows it. I married you because I loved you.'

'Loved me? You lie to me and in the same breath say that you love me.'

'I didn't mean to practise any deception, darling. Please *try* to believe me.'

'But you told me that Helena had married another man.'

'I believed that. Before God, I did. The note she wrote you was genuine.'

'She said it was forged.'

'She knows that's a lie.'

Nick began to pace the room.

'Who am I to believe? How can I believe in you? When you first came, you told me a long story about this woman for whom you were coming out to work. *That* was a lie and it seems to fit in with the other lies which Helena says you have been telling. I'm beginning to see things clearly. You just tricked me into marrying you, Toni.'

Toni kept her face covered. It was burning, although her body felt chilled and cold. She felt she was caught in a trap from which there was no escape. Her original lie made everything look so black against her.

'I didn't trick you, Nick. I loved you.'

'Love me? Don't keep saying you love me. It's a mockery,' he continued bitterly. 'You tricked me—I only wish to God Helena had arrived before I put that ring on your finger. Now we're tied up—and I despise you.'

His words seemed to break Toni's heart. She looked up at him, her face streaming with tears.

'No, no, Nick . . . don't say that.'

'I do. You've put me in a grand position! What about that wretched girl downstairs, rushing out here to me after a year's devotion. What must she think of me?'

Toni's lips twisted. A year's devotion! If only he knew the truth—how Helena had spoken about him—how she had sneered at his love.

'You're misjudging me, Nick,' she said. 'As I say, the whole thing's a dreadful tangle and from my point of view inexplicable. But I'm not as bad as you think. You must believe that Helena *did* break with you and say she was going to marry Bobby Deane. And above all

62

you must believe that I love you.'

'I don't,' he said savagely. 'I don't believe a word you say. When you told me Helena was finished with me, I vowed never to trust another woman. I was mad to trust you. Crazy! I wish to God I'd never seen you.'

He broke off suddenly and rushed out of the room. Toni sat rigid, staring at the floor. She heard him run down the stairs. She could hear his muffled voice as he began to talk to Helena. She could imagine his hideous state of mind, the agony which he must be suffering. And she had thought she would be able to make him happy—to help him forget the pain which Helena had caused him.

Toni looked round the bedroom. Nick's big, cool room which had been rearranged for them by the devoted Marie. Green silken curtains across the windows; cool green embroidered linen on the big bed in the corner. There were flowers everywhere—great bunches of scarlet and purple blossoms—brilliant, exotic flowers which Marie had brought from the garden. Their own room! Nick was right—it was a mockery—the whole thing was a mockery. It seemed impossible that a few hours before she had gone to her wedding like one in a strange, lovely dream; her whole heart aching with the desire to make Nick happy and with the knowledge that she would adore him for ever.

How could Helena have acted with such

incredible meanness and duplicity? And where had she gone now? What next did she intend to do? Well, she couldn't do much more. The harm was already irretrievable.

A sudden pang of misery shot through her body. The position was hopeless. Nick would never trust her again. Life for them both would be impossible. There was only one thing she could do. She must go away—go at once.

Crossing the room, she dragged a suitcase from the cupboard and began to pack.

CHAPTER FIVE

In the drawing-room, Nicholas Brendon talked with Helena and offered the apologies which, in his ignorance, he thought were due to her. She sat beside him on a sofa, a handkerchief to her eyes in an attitude of well-simulated grief. It was easy for Helena to cry. She could weep from sheer rage because she had arrived too late to prevent the marriage.

'I'm damned sorry, my dear,' Nick was saying. 'Heaven knows I can never offer you sufficient apology. But your note—Toni's story of your affair with Deane—your failure to turn up—you see how it was, how I was deceived?'

'Yes, I see,' Helena nodded. 'Toni has managed to ruin both our lives. Oh, Nicky, it's terrible. I feel I can't face it—to thick that *she* is your wife.'

Nick offered Helena a cigarette and lit one for himself.

'Look here, Helena. There are several things I want to know. First of all, when I stopped writing, why didn't you write me and ask for an explanation? I might have been ill.'

'That's true, but you see I expected a letter every day. When it didn't come, I took it for granted you were too busy to write. I was too proud to complain. I admit it.'

'Wasn't that very stupid of you? I'd never failed to write before.'

Helena looked away from his searching eyes.

'Yes, but I knew if you'd been ill, your partner would have wired me.'

'I told you he had died.'

'That was the letter Toni intercepted.'

'But why should Toni do a thing like that? It was dangerous—even criminal. If you'd got in touch with me it would have shown her up at once.'

'She took that risk.'

Helena seized the opportunity to cover her own weak points in the story by discussing Toni, and hurriedly continued:

'She was always a little mad. I think she had a strange, quite crazy desire to meet you. Your photographs and my stories of you used to fascinate her. She was determined to get out here and break things up between us and have a shot at winning you for herself.'

'But it's three weeks since I last wrote you, Helena. Why didn't you phone?'

'My dear Nick. I'm always "broke" and you know it. I can't afford Continental trunk-calls.'

Nick put a hand to his forehead in a puzzled way. He did not know which of the two women to believe. It was a monstrous position. Helena's reappearance and the fantastic story about Toni were so baffling that his mind would not cope with it all. Toni's story had seemed plausible. But then so was Helena's. And, breaking through his cloud of infatuation for Toni, he had to remember that Helena had once been engaged to him. He knew her well: What did he know about Toni? Nothing. She had come here with apparent proof of Helena's wish to break with him. That letter which Helena now said was forged (it was so easy to do that on a typewriter), and he had turned to her on the rebound. A man did mad, foolish things in moments of great disillusionment. But now Helena was telling him more about Toni than he knew.

'Do you know, Nick, she once tried to come between me and the manager of the shop where we both worked, merely because she was jealous that he had raised my salary and not hers. She tried to make mischief. She has a jealous nature. She was always jealous of my engagement to you. But I must say she took a frightful risk in going as far as this.'

66

Nick smoked on in grim silence, trying to puzzle it all out. He saw no real reason to disbelieve Helena. After all, so far as he knew, she had never lied to him or been unfaithful. But Toni had had every reason to lie. Helena said she was penniless: that she was shortly going to lose her job; that she was crazy to get married.

His cheeks burned duskily at that last thought. It was horrible to think that Toni was what Helena described her . . . almost a nymphomaniac . . . mad to get hold of a man she had never met, at any price. Yet that didn't seem possible. She had been so sweet, so reserved until he had made the first move towards her. If Helena was telling the truth, then it was certainly a rotten business for her.

The state of his mind was desperate. A month ago, he would have been madly excited at seeing Helena. He would have gathered her into his arms and kissed her as he kissed Toni. The sight of the slim, well-groomed figure, the satin-black head, the sparkling brown eyes would have meant everything on earth to him. But that feeling was dead. It had gone after the first bitter pain of disappointment in her had faded. Then Toni had come. Toni had transformed his life. She had taken Helena's place in his heart—found a deeper place than Helena had done, because they had more in common. Their mutual understanding of things; their interest in music and books which he and Helena had never shared.

His passion for Toni was more complete. Helena had always been a little cold and independent. She called herself sophisticated. Toni seemed simple, more child-like and much more generous. She was the one who wanted to give. She had been gentle and yielding and responsive to his passion. Like a flame, ardent, intoxicating in his arms. The thrill of watching the adoration in her golden eyes had roused emotions in him which Helena had never touched.

In fact, Toni had become his idol, the realization of all his dreams. And now that idol had crashed at his feet. And here he was, alone with another woman after three weeks of Toni's companionship—and that woman was the girl whom he had once regarded as his future wife.

A sudden pity stirred him when he saw Helena in tears. He took her hand between his and pressed it.

'Don't cry, my dear. It's the devil of a mess, I know. It's been so sudden. I can't realize it's all happened.'

Hope revived in her when she found that he had some of the old tenderness left for her. She might get him yet. She must. He was so much more handsome and attractive than he had been in England. *And he was rich.* She put a hand on his head.

'It's awful, Nick,' she whispered, 'simply

awful. I love you so, Nicky. Do you still love me?'

'Nicky' had always been her pet-name for him, the name she used when she was most affectionate. It made him feel uncomfortable as he heard it and felt her hand against his hair. He could not say that he still loved her; once love died, it could not be reborn.

He touched the back of Helena's hands with his lips and stood up. His face was white and drawn. He looked out of the window at the brilliant sunlight in the garden.

'I must be frank with you, Helena,' he said. 'I'm not in love with you as I used to be. You must forgive me. It's hard for me to readjust my emotions so quickly. You see—Toni has become everything.'

Helena broke out:

'It's unfair. It's cruel. Why should I suffer for Toni Kenyon's lies?'

'Toni Kenyon,' he repeated the name slowly, 'is now unfortunately, Toni Brendon.'

Helena stood up. Her eyes flashed.

'I won't let her take you from me. She will not.'

'The thing's done, Helena.'

'You must send her away—divorce her.'

'I can't do that.'

'It's impossible for you to keep her with you.'

Nick laughed.

'She won't have too good a time,' he said

grimly. 'Be sure of that.'

'That makes no difference to me. I want you. We were engaged so long, Nicky. Send her away—keep me here—you must.'

'It's too late, Helena. I've married her. Marriages can't be annulled without reason.'

'Isn't there reason enough?'

The argument went on. Helena began to fear that she would find it difficult to get Nicholas back. He was in a state of mind which bordered on the desperate. But she refused to admit defeat. He would probably be easier to deal with when he had got over the shock of the last hour. Finally, she allowed him to put her in his car and instruct the chauffeur to drive her to Mentone to an hotel.

'You'll see me tomorrow?' she asked.

He nodded.

'Yes. I'll come down to see you. I must have time to think things out—to make up my mind what is the best thing to do.'

She could see that it was useless prolonging the farewell. She touched his hand and bade him good-bye, her eyes full of tears.

Nick watched the car disappear out of sight. Then he returned to the house and went upstairs to Toni's room. He found her with her hat on. She was closing a suitcase.

'What do you think you're doing?' he said.

'Going away,' she said tersely. 'I can't stay here now. I know what you think of me.'

He slammed the bedroom door behind him

and stood with his back towards it.

'You're not going. You're staying here to compensate me for making a damned fool of myself.'

'Nick, you believe Helena rather than me! Well, you're entitled to. But you can't expect me to stay here.'

'Oh, but I do. I want you.'

'You can't want me,' she said hotly. 'It isn't possible.'

'Yes, it is. A man can hate a woman and still want her.'

For a moment they stared at each other in blind misery. Then he strode across the room and seized her in his arms. She felt his fingers grip her like a vice. Her head fell back against his shoulder, her eyes looked at him in terror.

'Nick,' she cried, 'let me go! You're mad.'

'Mad!' he laughed. 'Perhaps I am. But you'll have plenty of time to find that out. Remember, you married me. You belong to me. I'm not proud of my wife, but I'm going to keep her with me. I need something to relieve the monotony of my life in this place.'

Toni stood motionless, staring at him with wide, frightened eyes. Was this her lover of the past weeks—the man who had seemed so immensely in love with her, and treated her with such charming friendliness as well as a lover's tenderness?

'You don't know what you're saying, Nick. You must let me go,' she repeated.

'I'm sorry, my dear. You must grant me this one favour. You wanted my kisses—or was it my money? Well, you shall have the kisses. But on my terms.'

'I shall run away.'

He laughed and shook his head. It was a grim laugh.

'I shouldn't do that. The French police are not sympathetic with errant wives. They'd have you back tonight, before you'd got away a couple of miles.'

She gave an hysterical laugh.

'Isn't this a bit melodramatic, Nick? It's 1938 and you can't force a girl to live with you if she doesn't want to.'

He put his hands in his pockets and rocked to and fro on the tops of his toes.

'My sweet, you were always so *anxious* to live with me!'

She flushed hotly.

'I fail to understand you,' she said. 'If you despise me as you say you do, why not get rid of me as quickly as you can?'

'I've already explained. It's lonely here. You may be an adventuress, but you look lovely.'

'I think you're rather beastly.'

He shrugged his shoulders.

'We won't waste time in a slanging match.'

She struggled against the desire to cry, and laughed.

'Get Helena to relieve your loneliness. You've taken her word before mine.'

'It's a very curious thing,' Nick said, 'that I don't find Helena as exciting *that* way as I do you. But don't take it as a compliment, my dear child.'

Then, Toni burst into tears.

'You're cruel and impossible.'

'Stop crying, sweet,' he said. 'You'll spoil your complexion. Make yourself look your best. Put on something really attractive. We'll have a very pleasant evening in spite of Helena's bombshell.'

He went out of the room, laughing. It was a hard laugh which filled her with dread, and the expression on his face had terrified her.

She lay down on her bed, and tried to pull herself together. Food and drink were brought to her by Marie, but she refused to look at the tray. The old French maid was shocked to find her mistress in tears. She threw up her hands with an exclamation of dismay, then gathered Toni in her arms and tried to comfort her.

'It's impossible, Madame, that you should weep on your wedding-day. Where is Monsieur Brendon? I will call him.'

'No, no,' Toni shook her head. 'He's gone out. I don't want to see him. Please leave me, Marie. I want to rest—to think.'

Marie laid a hand on Toni's forehead and stroked back the thick golden hair.

'You're not well, *cherie*. Your head is burning. I must bathe it with eau-de-cologne.'

Toni lay like a dead thing with eyes closed

while Marie fussed about the room. It was true that her head was burning. It ached with a sharp pain which seemed to blind her. She felt incapable of argument. She only wanted to be quiet, to forget her own unhappiness and the misery which she had brought to Nick.

Marie brought the cologne and a bowl of iced water. Tucking up her sleeves, she set to work in her own practical way, soaking cotton-wool in the water and cologne, laying cool pads of it on Toni's burning eyelids.

'You're just over-excited, *ma petite*. Or perhaps it's a touch of our Riviera sun.'

Toni moved fretfully as the old woman smoothed her pillows and straightened the bed. She took the pads from her eyes and stared at Marie.

'It's my own fault. I lied to him. He found me out. And now he thinks I'm vile, despicable.'

Marie patted her hand.

'Don't you worry your pretty head. I'm sure it was only a foolish little lie. We all tell them at times. You must rest now. When Monsieur returns, you will feel better—you will talk to him and he will understand.'

Toni shook her head.

'I've tried to explain. It's no good. He won't believe me.'

'Of course, he will,' Marie insisted. 'M. Brendon is—how do you say it?—temperamental. He is easily upset but he always gets over it. Often he gets angry with me and then suddenly it is finished and forgotten. It will be the same with you.'

When Marie left her room, Toni lay back on her bed and tried once again to get some sleep. But tired though she was, she could not escape the torment of her thoughts. If only Marie were right! If Nick would return and understand and trust her.

Later Marie brought her a fresh tray with an omelette and some coffee. Toni refused the food but drank the coffee which was delicious. It seemed that after that, she slept for a little. When she awoke, it was dark. The villa was very quiet. Nick had obviously not returned. That meant he had gone down to the Club and dined there. Rising from her bed, she walked across the room. The curtains were drawn back from the window. The moonlit night was miraculously lovely. She stood there, staring out, her ears strained for the sound of a car.

She thought:

There was still time to escape from the house. She could easily walk through the woods to the Cap Martin Hotel. But on second thoughts she decided that it would be better to stay. It was just possible that Nick might return in a more reasonable mood; that she might be able to persuade him that it was Helena who had lied, and that *her* love for him was genuine. However wrong she had been to come out here in the first place, she would so gladly dedicate the rest of her life to him. If only he would believe that!

She stood by the window for the best part of an hour. Then she heard the sound which started her heart racing and drained the colour from her cheeks. The Packard was climbing the hill towards the drive.

She did not move. She had no lamp. She neither knew nor cared what she looked like. Her hair was wild and tangled. Her white dress crushed. She stood motionless, her eyes turned towards the door. She heard Nick come up the stairs to her room. The handle turned and the door opened The velvet darkness of the Riviera night was broken by a shaft of light from a lamp in Nick's hand, and now the room was flooded with light. He closed the door behind him, locked it and set the lamp on a table. Toni caught her breath as she saw him. He looked ten years older than the man she had married that morning. His face was worn and haggard.

He stood before her. He cast only the most cursory glance at her.

'Still in this'—he came nearer and touched her dress—'I should change into something more comfortable, if I were you, and make up that attractive little face of yours. I don't want to kiss any more tears away.'

'No,' she said, her eyes beseeching him. 'Wait until the morning—don't do anything tonight that you may regret—for your sake as well as mine.'

He flung back his head and laughed.

'Don't worry about me. I've given up having regrets. They don't pay.'

'Nick—please let us talk it all quietly out.'

'I don't want to hear any more lies. If I was the old-fashioned type of husband, I would thrash you. But I shan't do that. I don't want to spoil my wedding-night.'

'If only you knew the truth!'

'I know enough.' he said grimly. 'You made sure of marrying me. Very well. We're married, aren't we? Let's celebrate. I had some champagne in the Club. I'll open a bottle for you, now.'

She shrank back from him. She could see now that he was like one demented—not to be reasoned with.

'Not now, Nick.'

'Don't try to damp my ardour. I've been waiting for this moment.'

He made a sudden movement towards her and caught her in his arms. He felt the warmth of her body as she lay unresisting against him, the scent of her golden hair which had always stirred him. He had grown to love her fragile, child-like beauty. It had seemed sad and sweet. It called for a man's tenderness. But tonight he knew nothing but passion. The passion of a man who had been cheated and sought retribution.

He was not a lover who worshipped at the

77

feet of his bride. He was a tempest—destroying—desiring. Yet he knew that he still loved Toni; that if he died tonight with her kisses on his lips, he would always love her.

He felt her shudder in his arms, heard her give a muffled sob. He stretched out a hand and turned out the little oil-lamp. Through the shuttered windows, a shaft of moonlight slanted across the floor. Outside, the velvet beauty of the blue Mediterranean night enclosed the white house.

Toni put a hand against his mouth.

'Nick,' she said. 'for heaven's sake—'

'Heaven doesn't come into this,' he said and closed her lips with a kiss. 'Only hell . . .'

She did not appeal to him again.

CHAPTER SIX

Another brilliant morning dawned over Cap Martin.

In the drawing-room, Toni lay on a sofa and tried to forget the nightmare of the last twenty-four hours.

Her face was white and pinched. The heat seemed to exhaust her, drain her already lowered vitality, and she felt so utterly humiliated.

Last night Nick had defeated her. She had expected him to condemn, to blame her for having wrecked his life. She would have understood that and could have borne it. But she could not bear the attitude of tyrant which he had suddenly assumed—nor the fact that he seemed contemptuous of and indifferent to her suffering. During the night she had prayed that morning might bring her some consolation, that the bitterness in his mind and heart might lessen. But the sting remained and she could not drive it away.

She had now begun to realize that the position was hopeless. It was impossible for her to continue living with a man who had no respect for her. Such a marriage could only end in disaster. And how could her pride allow her to remain with a husband who was merely possessive—whose only interest in her was one of physical passion, and who did not wish for her friendship?

She lost all sense of time as she lay there, trying to evolve some reasonable plan for the future. She had told the servants that she wished to rest, and it was almost midday before she was disturbed by a knock on the door. Marie entered quietly and closed the door behind her.

'The English lady is outside, Madame,' she said. 'The one who was here yesterday. Do you feel well enough to see her?'

Toni raised her head from the cushions and ran her fingers through her hair.

'Yes,' she nodded; 'ask her to come in.'

She felt almost relieved that Helena had arrived. The sooner they thrashed things out the better. They must come to some decision. She could not endure another day in Cap Martin, knowing that Helena was seeing Nick and poisoning his mind with fresh lies about her, Toni. It would be so much easier to leave—to give Helena to him for good.

'Sit down,' she said, as Helena entered the room. 'Nick is out. I suppose you know that?'

Helena nodded. She had slept well and had dressed with more than usual care. The knowledge that she looked her best strengthened her for the attack which she expected Toni to make. She was clever enough to know that she had no defence. But she did not care. She had burned her boats. There could be no turning back. She must get Nick and get him quickly. If she failed now she must admit final defeat.

'My God,' she said, glancing at Toni, 'you look ghastly!'

'I feel it. But don't let that worry you. Helena, how could you have played a rotten game like this? It's unbelievable!'

Helena helped herself to a cigarette from a box on the mantelpiece and struck a match.

'Don't waste time cursing me, Toni. I made a mistake in throwing Nick over. I want him back and I intend to get him.'

'I realize that. But how do you propose to do it? He happens to be my husband.'

Helena blew out a cloud of smoke.

'He has no wish to retain that exalted position, my dear.'

'That's just where you're wrong. He won't give me up.'

'Don't be a fool,' Helena said irritably. 'You know damned well that he married you because he couldn't get me. I admit I made a mistake. I was infatuated with Bobby but I never stopped loving Nick. I still love him and I want him.'

'You never loved him, Helena. You just want his money.'

Helena shrugged her shoulders and laughed.

'What if I do? It's my own business.'

'It is also mine. I came out here with the intention of consoling Nick for your loss. When I married him yesterday morning, I had only one wish—to make him happy. I didn't care about his money. You know that's true, don't you?'

'I know nothing except that Nick once belonged to me and I want him again.'

'And you expect me to give you my blessing and leave, then hand you both an easy divorce!'

'Look here, Toni,' Helena said; 'do try to be sensible. Nick hates the sight of you now. You're perfectly well aware of it. Do you want to stay under such circumstances? Judging by your appearance, the first night of your marriage has hardly been a success!'

Toni felt the colour rise to her face at the reminder of last night. How could she ever forget the memory of those hours—of Nick's arms holding her—of his bitter, sneering voice saying:

'Heaven doesn't come into this . . . only hell.' He had said that, and meant it. And there could be no heaven for her in this house—only a sea of despair and disillusionment in which she must inevitably sink. She loved him. But he had taken Helena's word against her, and she realized that he despised her even while his lips were against her mouth. Helena was right. She could not stay with Nick now, and risk another night when he might force her to share that particular hell which the sharpness of his own disappointment had created for him.

She rose to her feet and walked to the window that opened on to the verandah. She stared miserably across the vivid flower-filled garden towards the farm. She remembered the days before Helena's arrival when she had stood by this same window waiting for Nick's return. Those had been wildly happy days which now seemed only a dream. She had been so content then in the knowledge that he would come to her eagerly, first as a friend and later as a lover.

'Do you intend to stay?' she heard Helena asking her.

Toni swung round to face the girl who had once been her friend.

'No, I don't. I shall leave here, and never come back.

'When?'

'As soon as possible. But before I go, I shall tell Nick, Helena.'

'Tell him what?'

'Everything. About my cheque and how you *sold* me your lover. I don't need to keep my mouth shut now. I have nothing more to lose. He shall know that you sold him, sold him for five hundred pounds. I have my cheque book, the counterfoil, my pass-book. He shall see that I gave you the money and know the reason why.'

Helena threw her cigarette out of the open window. Her eyes narrowed uneasily for an instant. Then she said:

'You can do what you darned well please, Toni. He won't believe you and if he does he'll probably be finished with the pair of us, and that won't help *you*.'

'I never dreamed anyone could be quite so ruthless as you, Helena.' Toni said slowly. 'You don't seem to care what misery you bring to people. You've managed to break me. Now, all I can say is God help Nick if he gets in your way!'

Helena turned away and walked towards the door.

'I don't think I'll waste time listening to

your sermons. I shall go back to my hotel. Nick's lunching with me.'

Toni winced. For a moment an overwhelming sense of loss, of injustice swept her. She felt she was near to losing her control. She made a sudden movement towards Helena and caught her shoulder.

'I could kill you for doing this. I was so happy—*he* was happy. You've ruined two lives with your treachery.'

Helena pushed her away.

'Cut out the dramatics, Toni. They won't work. You know what Nick thinks of you now—don't give me the chance to supply him with any more unpleasant details.'

Toni sat down on the sofa. Her head sank forward on her arms. She did not hear Helena leave the house. She was beaten. She could think of nothing but a desire to get away. She had been punished enough for the lies which she had told Nick. It was true she had done wrong, primarily, in buying the right to come out here to him. But beyond that she was guiltless. The punishment which Nick and Helena were inflicting on her now was out of all proportion to the crime which she had committed.

A sudden feeling of resentment began to grow in her. Why should she allow those two to hurt her like this. She revolted against the cruelty of fate. She began to tell herself that the intense and concentrated devotion which

84

she lavished on Nick had cast a spell on her. She had felt incapable of thinking clearly. But what Helena had to say—the realization that Nick was now believing in, confiding in Helena, acted as a stimulant to her tired brain. The knowledge that Helena had probably killed Nick's admiration for her for ever, urged her to new plans of action.

She walked to her bedroom and sat down before her dressing-table. A pipe lay beside her glass powder-bowl. She picked it up and fingered it mechanically. Nick's pipe. She remembered him throwing it there the last time he had been in the room. The memory of what he had said and done, rekindled her desire to show both him and Helena that they could no longer hurt her. She would find her passport and some money, and leave the house this afternoon.

As she began to collect a few clothes from her cupboard, she caught sight of her reflection in the long mirror. Helena had said that she looked ghastly. Well, she did! Her face was greyish and there were heavy, dark shadows under her eyes. Her lips were pinched and the fair hair clung damply to her forehead. She looked ill, old, she thought. But she would not let Helena—vile, treacherous Helena—rob her of her youth and beauty.

Then came the sound of a motor-car climbing the hill from the town. She jumped to her feet, dropped a chiffon dress which she had been about to pack and ran to the window. Was it possible that Nick had returned already? She felt sick with the idea of another scene with him. It would be more than she could stand. But no. It was not his car. She heard Marie's voice and the old woman's slow steps as she climbed the stairs: The next moment, Marie knocked on the door.

'*Monsieur* Soutro has called, Madame.'

Toni, her heart-beats slowing down, moved near the door.

'*Monsieur*—who?'

'*Soutro*, Madame. *Soutro.*'

Toni tried to think. Where had she heard that name? Ah, yes. Now she remembered. Garry Soutro was an Englishman who lived on the neighbouring estate. Nick had spoken of him once or twice as a good-looking fellow with a weakness for women which was always getting him into a jam.

Toni gave a twisted smile as she recalled Nick's words. She could remember quite a number of things that Nick had told her about Soutro. He specialized in comforting unhappy wives—that was one thing. Well, he might come in useful, be a blessing in disguise. She didn't want comforting—the kind of comfort she imagined Soutro could supply. But he would be someone to talk to. He might even suggest a job for her until she could save enough money for her fare to England. If she chose to make herself attractive she might win

86

his sympathy and understanding. She was being forced to fight with her back to the wall now. She could not afford to be selective in the choice of weapons.

'Ask M. Soutro to wait, Marie,' she said, picking up the chiffon dress again. 'Give him a drink and—run my bath.'

CHAPTER SEVEN

When Garry Soutro saw Toni walk into the drawing-room, half an hour later, he was staggered by her appearance. He had heard that Brendon had married an attractive girl, but he had not expected this radiant creature who smiled a welcome at him. He had been growing bored with waiting and had wished that he had gone straight to the Club for his usual game of bridge. But once he saw his hostess, he felt that he was compensated. This girl was a real beauty—and Soutro considered himself a connoisseur. He took her hand and looked into her strangely lovely eyes. They were burnt-gold under their dark lashes. Where the deuce had old Brendon found a wife like this?

'I'm sorry to have kept you waiting,' said Toni, shaking hands with him.

'Perhaps I arrived at an inconvenient time?'

'No . . . It is so nice of you to call.'

'I'm afraid it's a bit soon. I mean you've only just been married and all that,' said Soutro, smiling down at her.

A faint smile curved her lips. Mr. Soutro might be even more embarrassed, she thought, if he knew quite how recently she had been married to Nick!

'Please don't worry about that,' she said. 'My husband is out. I'm glad to have somebody to talk to.'

He did not say, as he would have liked to do, that he was delighted to find her alone. He took the chair she offered.

She sat down and they lit cigarettes. She found Soutro much as Nick had described him. A typical product of the Riviera. Handsome in his fashion, thin and almost foreign in appearance. Nick had told her that he believed Soutro had South American blood in his veins. The young man made little appeal to Toni either physically or mentally, but he was a witty conversationalist. At any other time she would have enjoyed his amusing commentary on life in the South of France.

He talked a good deal about the English residents—the narrow-minded, bigoted community who lived along the coast. He said they had little time for him, and he was not asked to the nice little dinner-parties held by the wives of retired army officers. That at least was a consolation, he said, laughing. It was more interesting to remain on the fringe of society and enjoy life.

He admitted to Toni that his reputation was not too good. There had been one or two incidents at the Club which the members had not forgotten.

'But I must stop talking about myself,' he finished with his curiously boyish smile. 'Tell me how you like Cap Martin, Mrs. Brendon. You must find it very quiet after London. Do you think you will be happy here?'

She winced at that name 'Mrs. Brendon'. God, how it hurt!

'I'm not staying,' she said suddenly, tersely.

Soutro stared at her.

'Leaving!' he repeated. 'But what about the farm? Is Brendon giving it up? I thought it was just beginning to pay?'

Toni walked to the table on which Marie had left the drinks. She refilled Soutro's glass and poured herself a gin-and-lime.

'Oh, Nick isn't leaving his lovely foxes.'

'But I don't understand,' Soutro began. 'You mean *he* is staying here and you're—'

Toni cut in:

'Yes. I'm leaving him for good.'

Soutro put down his glass and lit another cigarette. This was startling news, even for the Riviera, where things had a way of happening unexpectedly. He had imagined that Toni would be the usual blushing bride with a sickly infatuation for her husband. And here was a lovely and very self-possessed young woman who intended quitting immediately after her marriage! The Club *would* have something to talk about after he got there later on, Soutro thought excitedly.

He leaned towards her.

'I'm most terribly sorry, Mrs. Brendon. Naturally, I had no idea, otherwise I would not have come!'

Toni deliberately smiled at him.

'I'm glad you did. I feel I must talk to someone. These last hours by myself have been ghastly.'

He felt that this was the kind of conversation he understood, and he reacted to Toni's invitation gallantly. He touched her hand with his fingers.

'Tell me all about yourself,' he said softly, 'if you care to. Sometimes it helps.'

Toni did not know whether to loathe him or confide in him. It could do no harm if she told him her story, and he might be able to help her when she left the house. So, in a few brief sentences, the unhappy story was told. She admitted that she had come out to Cap Martin under false pretences, that she had lied to Nick Brendon in the first place. But she asked Garry Soutro to believe that the lie she had told had not merited the punishment which Nick was inflicting on her now.

'We were utterly happy,' she said, 'until Helena arrived.'

'Is Helena the girl you lived with in

London?' Soutro asked the question with intense interest. It was the most amazing tale he'd ever heard—the sort of thing one read in a dramatic book or saw on a film.

'Yes. The one who was engaged to Nick.'

'I see,' Soutro said, 'and when her boyfriend let her down, she came out here to try to get Brendon on the rebound?'

Toni nodded.

'That's right. She knew that I dare not tell Nick the whole story, and now she has made him loathe my name.'

'But if you run away—is that not an admission of guilt?'

'It may be, but I must go. I refuse to stay another night in this house with a man who feels nothing but contempt for me.'

Soutro rose from his chair and walked to the window. He was utterly disinterested in the beauty of this place. But in Toni Brendon he was more than interested. He could see that she had made up her mind. She was in the hard, unforgiving mood of a woman who had been turned down. What a fool Brendon had been to treat her as if she had been a common adventuress! But then, Soutro had always had contempt for the average man who played the role of injured husband. He could imagine Brendon being unbearably possessive and priggish. He had never been a close friend of his. It seemed to Soutro that if Brendon had treated the girl differently, with more understanding and less mistrust, she would probably have told him the whole truth.

He turned back to Toni.

'Where do you intend to go?' he asked.

'That's what I want to speak to you about,' she said on an impulse. 'I wonder if you could think of anywhere that I could stay until I get a job. I can't afford an hotel in Mentone.'

'Have you no money of your own?'

'Not a bean. I spent all I had on my ticket and clothes before I came out here.'

Soutro finished his drink.

Well, there's no need to worry about that. I can cash a cheque when I go down to the Club. But what we're going to do with you is a different matter.'

'Don't you know somebody in Mentone who would let me a room?'

'That's no good. Brendon would hear where you were, before morning. We must take you farther afield. If I know Brendon, he's the kind of fellow to leave no stone unturned to find you.'

'But he can't force me to return here.'

'No, but he can make things dashed unpleasant for you and for the people you're with.' Soutro gave a short laugh and added:

'Heaven help *me* if he finds I've had a finger in the pie!'

There was silence for a moment and then Soutro became aware that Toni was crying. He could see her slender shoulders quivering. She gave a little muffled sob and buried her face in her hands. He crossed the room and, kneeling beside her, put an arm around her. He felt a sudden wave of compassion for this girl. Brendon had certainly made a mess of things. Well, it would be his own fault if the fool lost her. The fellow needed a lesson in psychology. If he, Soutro, had had a girl like Toni for his wife, it would have taken more than a few lies to remove her from his arms.

'Don't you worry, my dear. I'm going down to the Club now. I'll find some way of fixing you up.' He took a large silk handkerchief from his pocket. 'Dry those tears and—but what's the matter?'

Toni's eyes had suddenly dilated, as though she had seen a ghost. Soutro removed his arm from her shoulder and turned his head. Nick Brendon was standing in the doorway. For a moment Garry Soutro was at a loss for words. Then he walked towards Nick and held out his hand.

'Hello, Brendon, how are you? I looked in to see you. Sorry you were out. I've been talking to your wife, and I fancy she's a bit upset.'

Nick ignored the outstretched hand.

'I'm sure you've been a wonderful comfort to her, Soutro. I understand it's your speciality. Now that I'm here, perhaps you will get out.'

Toni jumped to her feet and faced Nick. There was cold anger in her eyes as she looked

93

up at him.

'Why act like a stage hero, Nick? Mr. Soutro has only been trying to advise me. He's the only person who has said a decent word to me since yesterday.'

Garry Soutro walked towards the door, a trifle uneasily. He felt that he could do no good by staying. It would merely make things worse for Toni if he attempted to argue with Brendon. He didn't expect the man to believe what his wife said. He was obviously in a highly nervous condition.

'I don't suppose you'll understand, Brendon,' he said. 'That is quite natural. But your wife is telling the truth. If you don't try to believe and understand her, you're a bigger fool than I thought you!'

For a moment, the two men looked into each other's eyes. Nick opened his lips as though to speak. Then closed them again. Without a word, he opened the door and stood aside. Garry Soutro walked out.

Then Nick turned to Toni.

'You might consider my reputation before asking muck like Soutro to my house.'

'You're thinking a great deal about yourself,' she returned in a voice as cutting as his. 'Did it not enter your head that I might need someone to talk to?'

'Certainly. But if you want a companion, choose a more suitable one than Soutro. He's been chucked out of every house in Cap

Martin. I can't allow him to hang around playing the "Great Comforter" to you, my unhappy little wife.'

Toni gave a gesture of despair.

'Nick,' she said. 'You must see this position is impossible. Why don't you give me some money and let me go? Then you could go to Helena. You believe everything she says, don't you?'

'I have no reason to disbelieve her.'

'One day you'll know the truth.'

'Don't let's go over that again. You wanted to marry me. I see no reason why you should be allowed to back out and find fresh amusement.'

Nick crossed the room and poured himself out a drink. He knew that he had behaved like a fool before Soutro, that the Club would be seething with gossip about him tonight. But they could go to hell as far as he was concerned. It was pure bad luck that the one man who would enjoy creating trouble, should have chosen to come here when he was out. He regretted bitterly that he had decided to lunch with Helena.

The lunch had not been a success. Helena's constant abuse of Toni had irritated him. He had drunk more than was good for him. His head ached abominably, his throat was parched and sore. That was why he had returned early. He wanted to sleep, needed to get his mind working clearly once again.

When he had come in here and found Toni in Soutro's arms he knew he was near to losing all control. He had had to make a superhuman effort to keep himself from hitting the fellow. Of course the truth was that he was jealous. And his jealousy proved beyond all doubt that he still cared for this girl. The thought drove him mad. He had tried to dismiss Toni from his mind, and with every hour that passed he wanted her more. He wanted to take her in his arms and let her kisses help him to forget the lies she had told him. But that could only end in fresh failure and humiliation. In the morning, the knowledge of her deceit would return to drag him down to the depths again. His old feeling of contempt for her treachery would create another hopeless, wretched crisis.

He could never forget that she had allowed him to build a castle of dreams around her, then knocked them down. Nor that she had come to him with apparent sympathy and understanding when he was at his lowest ebb, under false pretences. He had made her his ideal, and in doing so, he had made a fool of himself.

He wondered why he would not do as she asked and let her leave. Perhaps it was to satisfy his vanity—or was it just a sadistic desire to hurt her, to make her suffer? Yesterday her silence and final collapse, and today her desire to leave him were in themselves definite admissions of her guilt.

How easy it would all be if he could feel capable of turning to Helena for consolation! Helena had always been in love with him. She had told him so time and again. And she was willing to return to him now—to marry him once he was free in spite of the fact that he had treated her so badly. It would have been a solution to his troubles if he could have felt the old flame burn. But he knew it would never work. His passion for Helena had died at the first touch from Toni's lips.

He finished his drink, and, putting the glass on the table, walked across the room.

'I'm going to get some sleep,' he said curtly. 'You might ask the boy to wake me in an hour.'

Toni stood like a figure of stone after he had gone. It was obvious that she could not reason with Nick in his present frame of mind. And his moods were growing worse. It was incredible how completely and hideously he had changed. She realized that he had suffered. But this afternoon, he acted almost as if he were demented.

There seemed only one thing she could do. She must get away while he slept. It meant going without her luggage, without money and—most important of all—without her passport. Her things were all in the room where Nick was resting. She dare not risk going up there, even when he was asleep. He might wake up, guess that she was trying to escape and stop her. Garry Soutro stood out in

97

her mind now as her only hope. The man to help her out of her difficulties.

A few minutes later she picked up the telephone and asked for the English Club.

'I want to speak to Mr. Soutro,' she said. 'No, don't give any name. He's expecting me to ring.'

The few moments that elapsed till Soutro answered that call seemed to Toni like an eternity. She put a hand to her head. She had scarcely been able to control her voice when she spoke to the exchange. Her heart pounded. If Nick came down now, she would be lost. If he found she was speaking to Soutro it would be the end, but at last she heard Soutro's voice:

'Hello! Who is it? Oh, you, Mrs. Brendon! I hoped you might ring.'

'Yes,' she said, 'I'm terribly sorry about this afternoon. I'm afraid things are impossible here. I've got to get away.'

His answer reassured her.

'Don't worry about this afternoon. Where's Brendon now?'

'He's asleep. That's why I phoned. Do you think you could possibly come for me and drive me down to the town?'

'Now?'

'Yes, straight away. It's my only chance.'

Soutro whistled to himself. Mrs. Brendon was certainly a fast worker and she had courage. Well, he would help her, if only to get a crack at Brendon. It wouldn't be the first time he, Soutro, had taken a risk with an attractive dissatisfied wife, and he hoped it wouldn't be the last.

'I'll be up in a quarter of an hour,' he said. 'I'll wait for you on the hill outside the gates. Good luck, you poor kid.'

Toni hung up the receiver. She could not think straight. 'Good luck,' Soutro had said. Well, she would need it! She could not imagine what the next few days would hold in store for her. She was without money, in a foreign country, with only this Garry Soutro—a man whose reputation was notorious—to look after her. She wondered if he would attempt to make love to her. If he would expect to kiss her. The idea of love-making made her shudder. She had no desire for any man's kisses—not even Nick's—at the moment. Though never again could there be room in her life for anyone else except the man from whom she was running away.

At the end of ten minutes, she could no longer bear the suspense of waiting. She stole to the front door to see if there were any servants about. There was no sign of Marie or the house-boy. Only one of the men on the farm walking away from the kitchen towards the fox-pens. Toni plucked up courage and ran—ran quickly. She ran lightly on the grass for fear that Nick might hear her footsteps. Not until she reached the road outside the estate did she begin to breathe more easily.

She was hot and out of breath when at last she saw Soutro's car approaching her. He drew up with a grinding of brakes and jumped out.

'Well done, my dear,' he said, holding open the door.

Wordless, white to the lips, she took the seat beside him. Her heart throbbed violently. There was a mist before her eyes. The car began to roll down the hill, out of sight of Nick's farm. And then a wild feeling, half of relief, half of despair, gripped her. She had escaped, got away. But when Nick woke to find her gone, what would he do? She covered her face with her hands and burst into a torrent of weeping.

CHAPTER EIGHT

Garry Soutro's car was running steadily along the white coast road between Mentone and Monte Carlo, when the near-side front tyre punctured and held them up.

Toni sat in the car, restless and nervy while Soutro changed the wheel. He cursed the heat, the dust and the fact that he had not brought a man to drive the car. But once the wheel was changed, he came back to Toni, smiling cheerfully.

'Rotten sort of job for this climate!'

Toni did not hear what he said. She glanced nervously behind her. Garry leaned over and took her hand.

'My dear,' he said. 'Don't fuss! I'll take care of you. Are you worrying in case this husband of yours follows us?'

'I'm sure he will.'

'Well, try to forget it just now. When we get to Monte Carlo we'll put our heads together, and see what's to be done with you.'

Toni was thankful that it was not a long drive. Soutro was trying to he bright. He kept up a running flow of trivial conversation. She tried to answer him, to let him see that she was grateful, but it was so hard to talk, and nothing that he said really comforted her. Her mind was leaden with misery. All she wanted to do was to be alone and say to herself: *'I mustn't think of Nick now. I'll think of him later, when it won't hurt so much!'*

It was almost six o'clock when they came into Monte Carlo. The streets were thronged with the usual smartly dressed crowds. The Casino steps were busy with inveterate gamblers who were leaving the afternoon session. Soutro pulled up outside one of the main hotels.

'Just cocktail-time,' he said. 'We'll both feel better after a drink. You deserve one certainly! Come along, little lady. I might say, as the song does, *"Lovely Little Lady"*, eh?'

She hardly noticed the flattery. She followed

Soutro into the lounge of the hotel, and they sat down in a secluded corner behind a row of palms. Soutro ordered drinks and pulled out his cigarette-case.

'And now,' he said, 'we can discuss our plan of campaign.'

Toni was silent until the waiter had set the drinks on their table. Then she said:

'Wouldn't it be wiser if I went to a smaller hotel than this one?'

Soutro shook his head.

'No. You're much less likely to draw attention to yourself in a place like the Hotel de Paris. If you go to one of the smaller ones, without luggage, they may ask questions.'

'It looks horribly expensive.'

'Don't worry about that,' he said, touching her hand. 'The main thing to think about is your passport. You can't move in this damned place without one.'

'What about the British Consul?'

'No good thinking about it until tomorrow. We'd better just eat, drink and be merry, tonight.'

'For tomorrow we die!' She finished with a miserable laugh.

'Don't you believe it,' he laughed back gaily. 'I've been getting people, including myself, out of jams all my life. I'll go and book a couple of rooms now.'

Toni gave him a swift look, and put down her cocktail-glass. Her heart sank.

'I don't think that would be wise,' she said quickly.

'Just as you wish. I'll get myself a shakedown somewhere else.'

She wondered if it was her imagination or whether there had been a sudden flash of disappointment in his eyes. Certainly, he had behaved most considerately to her up till now. Was it possible that he was going to reveal another side of his character to her tonight?

But Soutro was on his best behaviour and, as the evening wore on, Toni began to feel happier about him. No one could deny that he had charm, and he was generous to the point of extravagance. Nothing was too good for her.

They dined on the terrace of the hotel facing an exquisite, flood-lit garden full of giant palms and multi-coloured carnations. There were amber-shaded lights on the little tables outside the hotel and Chinese lanterns in the trees. Across the garden one could see the twinkling lights of ships in the harbour.

It was a still, hot Mediterranean night. Somewhere on the terrace a string orchestra played a waltz. One or two couples danced. All the gaiety, the sophisticated brilliance of the Casino-town was here.

Toni drank the champagne which Soutro had ordered. She made an effort to be a reasonably interesting companion. After all, he had treated her very decently. If he had not helped her to get away, she might still have

103

been at Cap Martin.

If only she could control her thoughts. Stop thinking of that other Casino town—San Remo—where she and Nick had first danced together. What was it he had said to her? *'We'll be another Astaire–Rogers combination!'* He had been so gay, so happy that day and she had been deliriously happy. She wondered if she could ever feel happy again, if she would ever again want to dance and sing.

She looked across the table at Soutro.

'I'm afraid I'm being very dull. But I feel so tired. My head aches abominably. Would you think me very rude if I went to my room?'

He rose and pulled out her chair for her.

'Of course, go to bed if you're tired, my dear child. I'll walk over to the Casino and lose some money, and tomorrow morning I'll phone you.'

Toni began to feel that this man was an angel in disguise. She held out her hand.

'I don't know *how* to thank you. You've been grand, Mr. Soutro. I shall never forget your kindness. I hope I shall be more amusing tomorrow.'

Soutro pressed her hand for a moment.

'I like you just as you are, and I hope we shall see a lot of each other,' he said gently. 'Good night, my dear, and try to sleep, and not worry. Brendan will never find you here.'

He watched the slim, golden-headed girl cross the terrace of the hotel. She was almost unbelievably lovely, he thought. And Brandon had let her slip through his fingers! The man must he a fool. But then, Soutro reflected, calling for his bill, there was a lot of truth in that saying that there was a fool born every minute in the twenty-four hours!

The office-clerk apologized to Toni when she asked for her key.

'I've had to give you a large double-room, Madame,' he said. 'This is a busy season. The hotel is very full. But I hope you will be comfortable.'

Toni nodded. She did not care about the room. All she wanted was to go to bed and sleep, to try to get some rest before the morning.

'I had to leave my home very hurriedly without luggage,' she told the man, as they went up in the lift. 'Can the maid get me a tooth brush and some things for the night?'

The clerk bowed.

'With pleasure, Madame. We have a shop in the hotel.'

He showed Toni to her room and, switching on the lights, promised that he would give her instructions to the chambermaid.

Toni looked around her. The bedroom was typical of the modern, luxury hotel. Rose carpet, striped-satin curtains, a conventional suite of polished sycamore. It was stiflingly hot in spite of the open french-windows, and an electric fan above the bed. Toni walked to the windows, drew aside the curtains and looked out. There before her lay the city of Monte Carlo with its white roofs and twinkling lights under the deep blue of the sky. She could hear the faint throb of a dance band from a neighbouring café. The Casino was a blaze of light. For a moment she wondered whether she should go there and risk the few hundred francs which she had in her bag on one wild throw. But that would be madness! Her luck was out just now and she would need every franc she could save during the next days. If she could get a job which would guarantee her some financial security in the future, how much happier she would feel! But her present position was hopeless. The money she had was not sufficient to keep her for a week, and there was no chance of getting a ticket for home. Nothing faced her but the grim necessity to earn her living.

Garry Soutro had hinted that she need not worry about finances, that he would settle her hotel bill. He was, she knew, a wealthy man. The money would make no difference to him. But, of course, she could not possibly allow him to pay for her. It would put her in an invidious position, and give him a hold over her which she would not for an instant tolerate.

She turned, as she heard a knock on the door. A page entered and laid a box on the bed.

'Some things for you to choose from, Madame. And I was asked to give you this note.'

Toni tipped the boy and tore open the envelope. The note was from Soutro.

Sleep well [*he had written*], I hope you will feel better in the morning, when I look forward to seeing you. I have decided to spend a few days in Monte Carlo so we must 'go places and do things'. I wonder if you realize how lovely you looked tonight? Brendon is a prize fool.

G.S.

Toni threw the letter on the bed and began to undress. This looked as though Garry Soutro might become difficult. She did not like the idea of him staying in Monte Carlo. Tomorrow she would suggest to him that it would be wiser if he returned to Cap Martin. But tonight she was too tired to worry any more about the situation. If she did not get some rest, she would be incapable of finding a job the next day.

She chose from the box a filmy pink nightgown, and a satin wrapper. The prices were not low, but she could not help that. She must have something to wear until she got her own clothes from Cap Martin.

Then she walked into the beautiful black-

and white-tiled bathroom which adjoined her room and ran an almost cold bath. She felt fresher after it, although her head still ached. Her nerves were at breaking point. She wondered why she had not remembered to ask the page to bring up a bottle of aspirins.

She tied the girdle of her dressing-gown round her waist and opened the bedroom door. Then she stopped dead. Her heart began to pound and her eyes dilated with sudden fear.

A man in grey flannels was there in the room, standing by the dressing-table. There was a suitcase on the floor beside him bearing the initials N.B. The man was Nick.

For an instant she stared at him speechlessly, too amazed even to say his name. He smiled at her, the cold cynical smile which she had grown to fear. In his hand he held a sheet of notepaper. She recognized it as the letter Soutro had just sent her.

Then she found her voice.

'*You!*' she said.

'Yes. I'm afraid this is a bit of a shock. I couldn't let you know I was coming. I might have phoned, but I told them not to announce me. As a matter of fact I said you were expecting me.'

She made an effort to pull herself together, to control her voice.

'I hoped you wouldn't try to follow me, Nick. I had to get away from you. It was the

108

only sensible thing for me to do.'

Nick twisted Soutro's note in his hand and threw it to her. She made no attempt to catch it. It fell at her feet.

'I congratulate you two on staying at different hotels. That was most discreet!'

'Don't be a fool, Nick. Soutro was merely a means to an end. I asked him to drive me here. There was nobody else to help me get away.'

'Where is Soutro now?'

'I don't know. I had dinner with him and then I came to my room. How did you find out that I was here?'

Nick Brendon laughed.

When I found you had gone, I guessed Soutro would be in it. I was positive you'd come to Monte Carlo. I made up my mind to search the whole damned place. Then I saw his car parked outside this hotel, well . . . the rest was easy.'

'What are you going to do now?'

He kicked the suitcase on the floor.

'I may as well stay here with my wife. It's too late to go home.'

Toni looked up at him blindly.

'For God's sake, Nick, leave me alone. I'm tired. Talk to me in the morning, if you must. But let me have some peace.'

'Peace at any price, eh? Even at the price of my aching heart? But you wouldn't be so unkind, surely, my sweet!'

Toni heard his words as if from a distance.

A sudden mist came across her sight. She made an effort to steady herself, but it was too late. She knew that she was going to faint.

Nick caught her as she swayed. He picked her up in his arms and laid her on the bed. She was as slender, as light as a child, and her face scared him a little. It was so ashen, so drawn. For an instant he was remorseful. The anger vanished from his eyes. He felt the old, bitter pain strike his heart. The pain which was always there when he acknowledged his love for her. He had followed her here this eveing, in a mood of blind anger. If he had found her with Soutro, he would probably have lost his last vestige of control and wanted to kill Soutro—or Toni—or both of them. But she was here alone. A pale, scared-looking slip of a girl. He could not be jealous. He could not even reproach her for leaving him. He found a glass of water and a towel and began to bathe her forehead gently, tenderly. Presently she stirred and opened her eyes. She looked up at Nick and gave a little cry.

'Please,' she whispered. 'Leave me alone. I'm only tired. I'll be all right in the morning.'

Nick was silent for a moment. He laid down the glass and towel. Crossing to the window, he stared down at the lighted streets. The hot air beat against his face.

'Just as you wish,' he said. 'I'll get another room.'

'Thank you, Nick.'

'You're sure you're not ill. You fainted, you know?'

'I'm quite all right now, thank you.'

He turned and walked slowly to the door. He did not even look towards the girl on the bed.

He said:

'I'll come for you in the morning. We'll drive home and then I'll tell you what I meant to say tonight. I advise you to leave a message for Soutro. Tell him that you've gone. It would be unpleasant if I met him here.'

Then he was gone, and the door had shut behind him before she had time to answer. She lay back on the pillow, the tears drying on her cheeks. Strange, unaccountable man! He had been almost kind just now. When she had first recovered consciousness and found him bathing her head, she had seen in his eyes a flash of the old tenderness; the love which she had known before they were married.

And then—as suddenly as he had come here—he had gone again, leaving an impression almost of sadness—something very lost and alone. But what would he say to her tomorrow? What could he say that would help either of them now? It was too late. She felt that she had lost the real Nick whom she had adored, and who had adored her, for ever.

CHAPTER NINE

That following night, Helena Lane sat in the lounge of her particular hotel at Mentone and fumed against the fact that Nick and Toni were still together.

Helena had done everything in her power to separate Nick from his wife. But he seemed adamant about his decision to remain with Toni. He despised her, he had admitted that much to Helena. But Toni was his wife. It was his duty to stay with her. When they lunched here yesterday Nick had been kind, even charming, to Helena. He told her repeatedly how sorry he was that she had arrived too late to stop his marriage. He had admitted that he had unwittingly let her down, and he seemed genuinely anxious to console her. He even insisted upon paying for her hotel bill, and offered to finance her return fare to England.

Helena accepted the money for the hotel gladly enough, but refused the return-ticket. She was determined to stay in Mentone as long as possible. For the first time in her life she was falling in love with Nick! He was more attractive than he had ever been. The years he had spent on the Riviera had given him a glamorous sophistication which he had lacked in London. If only she could get rid of Toni, she believed that she would still have a chance of getting him back. She would play on his sense of honour—towards her—amplify the fact that he owed a duty to her, rather than to Toni.

As for the emotional side of it—well, once he had adored her. Her brown eyes and satin-black hair had meant everything to him. She ought to be able to make him adore her again.

At six o'clock Helena rose from her chair in the lounge and walked to the cocktail-bar. It was the most cheerful spot in the hotel. Every night it was filled with a cosmopolitan crowd. Helena loathed being alone and preferred the bar to any other room in the place.

This evening there was only one free stool by the circular bar. Helena seated herself gracefully upon it and ordered a gin-and-Italian. When the barman returned with her glass, he leant across the counter towards her.

'Excuse me, miss. The gentleman in the corner wonders if you would care to join him.'

Helena glanced towards the table which the barman indicated with some amusement. She recognized a tall Englishman, of heavy build and florid complexion, to whom she had spoken in the lift that morning. He smiled as she looked round and pointed to a vacant chair at his table. Helena left her stool and walked across the room. She was not impressed by the man's appearance, but with an insolence typical of her, she decided that there was no reason why he should not pay for her drinks.

The man rose to his feet as she joined him.

'Good evening. I hope you don't mind me sending you that message?'

Helena smiled under her long lashes.

'It's very kind of you. I hate sitting by myself.'

After a few drinks and cigarettes, it was fairly obvious to her that this man was not a desirable companion. She soon knew all about him. He told her that his name was Victor Black, and that at one time he had managed a nightclub in London.

It was a club which Helena remembered. Bobby Deane had taken her there before it was raided and closed down.

Now he was in control of a chain of clubs along the French and Italian coasts.

He had money and liked to display the fact. He wore a diamond ring on his little finger and a pearl tie-pin. He was not the type to amuse Helena.

'Are you staying here for long?' she asked, without real interest.

'That all depends,' he said, taking a cigar from a pig-skin case. 'I'm looking for new talent. Up to date I haven't been very successful.'

'What exactly do you mean by "talent"?'

Victor Black broke the band of his cigar with a well-manicured thumb-nail.

'In my job it means beauty, a good pair of

legs and an idea of rhythm.'

'Is training not necessary?'

'Not as long as the girl knows how to dance. Why do you ask me?' he said with sudden interest. 'Don't tell me you're wanting a job. Now when I saw you, I thought: "That's a damned handsome kid if ever there was one"!'

Helena shook her head. She certainly did not want a job in one of Mr. Black's troupes. She had every intention of staying in Mentone with Nick. But Toni wanted to get away; Toni had said that she needed work which would bring her in enough money to support herself. And Helena remembered that Toni used to dance in amateur theatricals. As for looks— she was pretty enough.

'Where would you want this girl to work?' she asked.

'Just across the Italian border. In San Remo.'

'And for how long?'

'Not less than three months. My girls have to sign a contract to that effect.'

Helena leant back in her chair and lit another cigarette. Her mind began to work swiftly and excitedly.

If she could get Toni out of the way for three months, she, Helena, would have every opportunity to win Nick back. But she would have to work carefully. If she introduced Toni to Victor Black and Toni had any idea that there was an ulterior motive behind it, she might not put her signature to the contract.

'Perhaps you know of someone who might be suitable,' Victor Black suggested, looking at Helena with some eagerness. 'If you do, it would be to your advantage, my dear girl. I mean I will give you the usual agent's fee.'

Helena smiled. Agent's fee! She would willingly pay the man if he would guarantee to get Toni into Italy.

'It's just possible,' she said, 'that I may be able to help you. I do know a girl who came out here a month ago. She married a man in Cap Martin. Things have gone wrong. She wants to leave him. But she has no money, and needs a job.'

'Would she do cabaret work?'

'I think so.'

'Pretty?'

'A blonde—considered divine by some men!'

'Would she sign on?' Black was more than ordinarily interested now. He liked blondes.

'It depends,' Helena said, 'upon the cabaret—and on how much she knew about it.'

Victor Black shrugged his shoulders.

'Our place in San Remo is—what shall I say?—gay but quite respectable.'

Helena looked thoughtful. She imagined that Black's idea of respectability might not coincide with Toni's. But if he could persuade her to sign the contract, to get away, the future would look after itself.

'Is it a straightforward contract?'

'Quite. As I say, the girls sign up for three months. We pay them the equivalent of three pounds a week.'

'Have you by any chance got some papers with you?'

Black nodded, and, taking a document from his inside pocket, handed it to Helena.

'There you are. That's my contract. But I doubt if you'll be able to read it.'

Helena glanced at it for a moment before she handed it back. The contract was in Italian.

'It means nothing to me,' she laughed. 'And it will be equally unreadable to Toni.'

He looked at her curiously.

'I'm sorry it isn't going to be you, my dear. But tell me more about this girl. When and how can I get in touch with her? And what about the husband? Is he likely to make trouble?'

'He certainly is. But he doesn't need to know anything about it. I will see to that. How soon do you want your new dancer?'

'The sooner the better. Tonight if it is possible.'

Helena tapped the edge of the table with her fingers. If she could get Nick to come down here this evening it would be easy for Black to drive up to Cap Martin and interview Toni. She imagined that Toni would soon make up her mind if she liked the sound of the job. She only wished that Black looked more prepossessing.

'I tell you what,' she said suddenly. 'I'll ask the husband here tonight. If he comes, you can go over to see Toni. Toni Brendon is her name—by the way—but you'll have to work carefully. If she doesn't like your contract, we'll be finished.'

'Most girls would jump at the job and the money.'

'Well, I hope Toni does,' Helena said, rising to her feet. 'If you wait here, I'll come back and let you know the plans.'

She crossed the bar and, entering the telephone box in the hall, put a call through to Nick's house.

Marie answered.

'Allo! Allo!'

'Is Monsieur in?' asked Helena.

'Oui, *Mamselle.'*

'Ask him to speak to Miss Lane.'

A moment later came Nick's voice.

'You want me, Helena?'

'Yes, Nicky. I must see you. Could you possibly jump into your car and come down tonight?'

'What's the matter?'

'Just the reaction of the whole affair, I suppose. I feel so miserable. I think I'll go mad if I don't have someone to talk to.'

Nick hesitated for a moment. He was tired. The last thing he wanted to do was to go out.

But he felt sorry for Helena, and always a trifle guilty about her. It must be rotten for her down there by herself. Yes, he would go down to her and try, once again, to persuade her to return to England.

'Right, Helena,' he said. 'I'll run down for a drink, my dear.'

'When?'

'Now, before dinner. I'll be with you in half an hour. Will that do?'

'It'll be fine, Nicky darling. Thank you.'

Helena hung up the receiver. Her heart beat violently. If Victor Black played his hand properly now, Toni would be gone by the time Nick returned home.

Black looked up at Helena, as she returned to his table.

'Well, what's happened?'

'I've fixed it. My friend is coming here now. He'll arrive in about twenty minutes. Then you can go up to the house and see your blonde.'

'How do I get there?'

Helena gave him directions. She advised him to be as quick as possible. Nick had sounded tired over the telephone, and she might not be able to persuade him to stay down here for long.

'Make your job sound as attractive as possible to Toni. And be sure you don't mention my name,' she said. 'If she asks who sent you, you'd better say somebody you met in Mentone. Tell her you don't remember the

119

name.'

Victor Black looked doubtful.

'Don't you know a name I could use? It would sound better.'

'Yes, I do,' Helena said suddenly. 'Say you met a friend of Garry Soutro's. That will satisfy her.'

Victor Black took out a notebook and wrote down the name. It meant nothing to him. He knew nobody here. But if it would help matters with the little blonde, so much the better. He began to look forward to his interview with Miss Toni. It was time they had fresh beauty in the San Remo troupe. High-time!

CHAPTER TEN

At the time Helena had telephoned to Nick, Toni was sitting with her husband in the lamp-lit drawing-room of their house. He was not talking to her. He was busy at his desk with business correspondence, connected with the farm.

Now and then she glanced at him and thought how utterly she loved him like that, sitting in his leather chair with a cigarette in the corner of his mouth and his forehead wrinkled as he wrote his letters.

He looked more like the man she remembered during her first weeks at Cap

Martin. But he was not that Nick by any means. He had been silent and morose since he had brought her back from Monte Carlo this morning.

When he called for her at the hotel after breakfast, she had tried to persuade him to stay until she could find a job. She argued that there could be no possible happiness for either of them if she returned to Cap Martin. It would only mean more misery.

Nick refused to agree with her.

'I don't expect you to be the wife I had hoped for. But you can help to make life easier for me. I need a woman to run my house,' he told her.

'You could get a housekeeper.'

Nick laughed.

'My dear. You made an excellent housekeeper. We got on very well together before we were married. You can return and take up your old duties again.'

Toni decided that she would make a final attempt to live with him. He certainly appeared more reasonable, more tolerant. If he would forget the agony of the last days, they might be able to settle down. She might eventually prove that she had his interests at heart, that she had always wanted to help him.

She left a note at the hotel desk for Garry Soutro.

Thank you [*she said*], for your kindness

121

to me yesterday. I have decided to return to Cap Martin. I think it is best. I'm sure you will understand, when I ask you not to try to see me.

Toni.

She was thankful that she got away from the hotel before Soutro called. She knew that Nick hated him and she dreaded a scene between the men. But Nick had the car round to the hotel by ten o'clock. They were back at Cap Martin by the time Soutro was due to meet her.

Nick left her after lunch and did not return until late afternoon. She knew that he was making an attempt to act more normally, to regain some of his old control. But she found it difficult to believe the change that had come over him. He seemed hard, embittered. She felt almost frightened of him this evening.

She looked up from the book she was reading as she heard steps on the verandah. There was a knock on the door and Nick rose from his desk with a curse.

'Who the devil is that?'

The door opened and Pierre, the head kennel-man came in. In his arms he held a silver-fox cub.

'I'm sorry to trouble you, Monsieur,' he said to Nick. 'The old vixen has had a bad time with her litter. I think I can manage to save most of them, but this little fellow is pretty weak.'

Toni jumped to her feet and ran across the room.

'Oh, Nick!' she cried. 'The darling! What can we do for it? Look, it's cold, shivering!'

Nick took the cub from Pierre and held it under a lamp.

'It's pretty far gone. But we might try some brandy. Get some cognac and warm milk, Toni. And an old blanket.'

Toni went to the kitchen and told Marie to heat some milk. When it was ready, she returned to the drawing-room and gave it to Nick.

He mixed a few drops of brandy in the saucer and, giving her the cub to hold, opened its mouth.

'Taste that, old boy,' he said. 'It's real Napoleon brandy. We're spoiling you!'

Toni looked up anxiously.

'Is there any chance for him, Nick? Do you think he may live?'

He wrapped the cub in the blanket which Marie had brought and gave it back to Toni.

'It's impossible to say. I hope so. You hold on to him and keep him warm. I must finish these letters.'

He sat down at his desk and tried to finish his letters, but he found it difficult to concentrate. His eyes kept turning towards the mirror which hung on the wall above the desk. He could see Toni's reflection in the glass. She was holding the cub in her arms, whispering to it and playing with the tips of its small pointed ears. Pain stabbed him at the thought that he might have seen her thus, with a baby in her arms.

He thought how lovely, how innocent she looked. It was impossible to believe that she could be guilty of deceit. She looked incapable of wrong-doing. There seemed something pure and ethereal about her this evening. She was like the painting of the Madonna in the drawing-room.

He wanted her more intensely then he had thought it possible to want anybody. Looking at her, he wondered why he did not go to her, ask her forgiveness for his past behaviour: why he did not ask her to help him forget the misery of the last days. He knew that she was the only woman in the world who had the power to make him happy. Why the devil in him—the devil of jealousy—forbid him to say what was in his heart?

He put down his pen and, crossing the room, sat down beside her.

'You'll spoil the little brute,' he said, taking the cub from her arms and laying it on the floor in its blanket.

She laughed quite gaily, and bent over the small animal.

'It's so sweet, Nick. I know I shall never see a silver-fox fur in a shop without thinking of it. It seems a shame to kill them. I shall never wear a silver-fox tie or cape as long as I live.'

He ruffled the cub's coat with his hand.

'You'll never see this one in a shop. It's got a rotten coat.'

Toni gave a little cry of delight.

'Then you can keep it with you? Have it for a pet?'

'If I want to. But it doesn't do to make pets of animals—or human beings. They let you down in time. A full-grown fox can be dangerous and as treacherous as a woman!'

She gave him a startled look. The tone of his voice had suddenly changed. It sounded so embittered. What a fool she had been to return with him this morning. He had promised her then that he would not make her conscious of her position as his wife; that he would demand nothing from her. She had believed him. He had seemed more normal, more like the old Nick. But tonight she could see that the devil was in him again.

He moved towards her, and for a moment she thought he was going to catch her in his arms. Instead, he laid a hand on her shoulder and said in a curious voice:

'I want you to kiss me, Toni.'

The colour drained from her face. She drew away from the cub and stood up. She made an effort to control her voice.

'Why ask me to do that, Nick? You know what you said this morning. That if I returned, you would treat me as your housekeeper. Kisses did not come into it.'

'You were my housekeeper once before. That didn't keep you from kissing me.'

'You told me that you would try to forget those days.'

'I said I would forget our *marriage*. I have nothing but the most pleasant recollections of you as my housekeeper.'

'Don't be a fool, Nick. Why did you persuade me to come back with you? Why did you make things so difficult? You must have known it would end in trouble.'

He made a sudden movement towards her—and then his arms were round her, his lips were against her cheek. He kissed her face, her hair and finally her mouth.

She made no effort to get away from him. She was utterly passive, not knowing whether she loved or hated this queer, unnatural man. She whispered:

'Must you do this? Must you act like a schoolboy?'

Nick released her. He laughed.

'You certainly have changed, my dear. Have I lost all my attractions for you?'

She did not reply. She knew it would be useless to protest. Nick was in one of those moods which she had learned to dread. If she argued with him now he would not listen. The devil in him controlled his reason.

She watched him cross the room. He stood before the gramophone. He opened the lid and put on a record. It was a gay dance-tune.

She felt she would scream if she had to listen to it. Then the sudden shrilling of the telephone in the hall eased the tension. Nick turned off the music. He walked out without looking towards her.

She heard him answer the call, heard him mention Helena's name. She did not care. Nothing seemed to matter. Then he went upstairs to his room and shut the door.

When he came back she was quick to notice that he had put on a dark, wine-coloured silk shirt and tie. His hair was slickly brushed. She thought that he looked amazingly young and attractive. But there was no youth in his eyes when he looked at her—only hostility.

'I'm going down to Mentone,' he said. 'Helena wants to see me urgently.'

Her heart sank. So it was for Helena he had made himself look like this! She picked up the cub and held its head against her cheek.

'All right.'

Nick stared at her bowed head. It was sheer gold in the lamp-light. She looked as slender as a child in her white linen dress.

'I wonder how any woman can look so innocent,' he thought, 'and be so rotten!' Aloud he said:

'I shan't be long. What time is dinner?'

'Half past eight. But why don't you dine with Helena? I'm quite happy here alone. I've got plenty to do.'

'It would be unkind to leave you alone the

first night you're back.'

'If you wanted to be kind,' she said bitterly, 'you would let me go away. All I ask is to be allowed to make a new start somewhere, become independent and find some sort of happiness. There's nothing to keep me here.'

He shrugged his shoulders.

'You're not exactly flattering. I assure you that I'm as good a lover as Garry Soutro.'

Toni did not stop to think. She was only conscious of blinding anger. She raised her hand and hit him across the face.

'I despise you for that, Nick!' she said in a choked voice. 'How should I know whether Garry Soutro is a good lover or not? I only know that he has treated me with more respect, more decency than you've done since Helena came out here.'

Nick put his fingers to the cheek she had struck. His eyes were expressionless.

'I'm sorry,' he said. 'I should have said I can be as good a *companion* as Mr. Soutro.'

But it was too late. Toni's control snapped. She flung wild, bitter words at him.

'You're no companion for any decent woman, Nick. You've insulted me as though I were a crook. You've tried to break my spirit just to satisfy your injured pride. And you very nearly succeeded. I used to love you, admire you. In those days you were able to hurt me, but now I don't care any more, and you can't be hurt by someone who means nothing—

128

simply nothing at all!'

Nick did not answer. For a moment he stared at her, then he crossed the room and shut the door quietly behind him. She heard the car throb outside and knew that he had driven away. She was alone. But not more lonely than when he was with her. They were entirely removed from each other. There could be no basis of understanding. How he hated her! Hated and desired her, too.

It was very still in the house. Through the long open windows leading on to the verandah she could see a great yellow moon. The mosquitoes hummed incessantly. A brown owl hooted from the bottom of the garden.

It seemed to Toni the most bitter and tragic moment of her life. Once again he had turned to Helena. And Helena was still fighting for him. She would get him in the end.

Toni buried her face in her hands. She did not cry. Her tears seemed to have dried up. But she was racked with an utter sense of despair. In an hour he would be back. He would taunt her and hurt her, destroy her afresh. And she loved him so. Even he could not utterly destroy that love.

'Nick,' she whispered. 'Nick!'

The sound of footsteps on the verandah roused her. She supposed it was one of the servants. She raised her head. Then she gave a little cry of surprise. A man walked into the drawing-room. A man with horn-rimmed glasses, carrying his hat in his hand. When he saw Toni, he paused and bowed.

'I must apologize for this intrusion,' he said. 'I saw you standing by the window, so I walked in. You are Mrs. Brendon?'

Toni gave a nervous laugh.

'Yes. And you?'

'My name's Black. Victor Black.'

'You gave me a fright. We don't get many callers up here. Are you a friend of my husband's?'

Black shook his head.

'No, I don't know him. I'm here on business.'

'Business with *me*?'

'Yes. Let me explain. I met a man in Mentone who told me that you wanted a job. And I've got one open for you. That's all.'

'Who was the man?'

Victor Black shrugged his shoulders.

'I don't remember his name. He said he knew a friend of yours called Soutro. Is that right?'

Toni nodded.

'Garry Soutro. Yes, I know Mr. Soutro. I did tell him the other day that I needed a job. I want to make some money. I must confess.'

Black stared at Toni. That girl down at the bar had been right. Toni Brendon was a real beauty, a true blonde. If he could get her to San Remo, his stay in Mentone would not have been in vain. She was ideal for the job. He was agreeably surprised. He had put hundreds of dancers through his hands, but this fair-haired, golden-eyed girl gave him a new thrill.

'The fellow told me you wanted work, so I thought you might be suitable in my place.'

'Sit down and tell me what kind of work you are offering,' said Toni.

Black took a cigar from his case, and seated himself on the sofa.

'Cabaret. I manage a string of shows along the coast. I want a dancer for my place in San Remo.'

'I've never done any professional dancing.'

'That doesn't matter. You have the looks. I'll teach you the rest.'

Toni lit a cigarette and reflected. A strange sense of excitement began to steal over her. She wanted to think, to have time to make a decision. She could not say that she liked this man. She was not inspired by his appearance. He was flashy, over-dressed. A poor type of man. But he offered a means of escape. That attracted her. Last night she had told Soutro she wanted a job in order to save enough money with which to return to England. Now she wanted more than ever to escape from the hell that Nick created for her.

'How much money would I make?' she asked.

'Three pounds a week and your expenses,' Black said glibly, quoting a pound over his usual offer. 'You could live with the other girls.

131

I supply the props for the work.'

Toni made a wild calculation. Three pounds and all expenses! Much more than she had made in London. If she stuck the job for six weeks, she would be able to buy her return ticket. But she would have to get away from here before Nick returned. Nick, who for sheer devilment would refuse to let her take this job.

'If I accept your offer I shall have to leave tonight,' she said breathlessly.

Victor Black smiled. So far as he was concerned the sooner she was at San Remo the better.

'That suits me, my dear. I'm going back there now, by car. I can take you with me. You think you'd like to work for me, eh?'

For a moment she hesitated. She knew nothing about this man. He was quick to guess what lay in her mind, and pulled out a card and handed it to her.

'You can phone the police at San Remo. They'll tell you my place is above-board.'

Her fears were set at rest. She said:

'I need the job. I'll come with you. Do I have to sign a contract or anything?'

Black concentrated on the end of his cigar.

'We give the usual contract—a mere formality. But there's no time for that now. We can see to it tomorrow. I'm late. You'd better go and pack. Don't forget your passport.'

Toni ran up the stairs to her room. She pulled a few clothes from the wardrobe and flung them into a suitcase. She found her passport, and a bag with some money in it. She did not stop to look round the room. She only wanted to get out. To forget this bedroom and the nightmare of the past.

The last time she had run away, helped by Soutro, Nick had followed and brought her back. But this time she knew, somehow, that he would not follow. He would let her go. That last flight had been wild and indiscriminate. After all, it could be misconstrued—allowing a perfectly strange man to take her to an hotel in Monte Carlo for no apparent reason.

This time there was a reason. She was going to a job. She need not fear that Black was a charlatan, no matter how she disliked his personality. He had shown her his card, and to prove that he was genuine had assured her that she could ring up the police. There was nothing to be afraid of—nothing. Particularly as Soutro had sent him. Soutro was a bad man where women were concerned—an impudent cavalier kind of fellow. But at heart he was kind. Sending Victor Black here had been an act of kindness on his part for which one day she must thank him.

She wondered what Nick would think when he came back to find her gone. Perhaps relieved that he had got rid of her. Perhaps he felt that it would be for the best for him to break with her finally. And there was always—Helena!

Toni locked her suitcase, took a last bitter look round the room then walked downstairs and called for Marie.

The old woman stared at her.

'All dressed up? And with a bag? Where are you going, *hein*?'

'I'm going to get a job, Marie. I can't explain to you but it is impossible for me to remain with Monsieur.'

Marie's eyes narrowed.

'Another tiff, *hein*?'

'Call it that if you like,' said Toni with a short laugh, 'but this time I'm not coming back, Marie, and I want you to tell him so and not to bother to find me.'

Marie reflected. In a way she had a certain affection for this young girl who had come so tempestuously into the life of her beloved Monsieur Brendon. On the other hand too much had been going on here—too much altogether. There was never any peace. Always troubles. Monsieur had been happier when he was alone. Marie clicked her tongue and eyed Toni a trifle slyly:

'*Eh bien!* I'll give your message.'

Victor Black came out into the hall.

'Ready?'

'Yes,' said Toni breathlessly.

Muttering to herself, Marie returned to her kitchen. Another man! What sort of behaviour was this? Far better was Monsieur rid of his wife. Far better if she, Marie, gave him no

134

message tonight—*no message at all.* And far, far better if he never saw her again.

In the drawing-room Toni bent over the little silver-fox cub which was curled up asleep in its blanket.

She touched its head.

'Good-bye, little pet. I hope Nick will take care of you.'

Then she turned, left the room and joined Victor Black. She was horrified to find that tears were rolling down her cheeks.

CHAPTER ELEVEN

Nick Brendon returned to his house at half past eight. He was in a difficult, angry mood. His nerves were jumping. He had spent the best part of an hour with Helena. She had looked unusually attractive and appealing this evening. Those magnificent eyes of hers had filled with tears when she looked at him. She had even spoken kindly of Toni, and, man-like, he was easily influenced by a pretty woman's subtlety. It made him furious to think that Toni had created such havoc for them both.

By the time he had reached home, there was little softness left in his heart for Toni; his eyes were moody, his mouth a thin, hard line.

'Toni!' he called.

There was no answer. The lamp was still

135

alight in the drawing-room, but the room was empty.

He went up to the bedroom. Perhaps she was resting before dinner. There was no light upstairs. He struck a match and looked round the room. The bed was turned down, but it had not been slept in.

'What the devil?' he muttered under his breath. 'Where is she?'

He ran downstairs again and shouted for Marie.

'Have you seen Madame?'

The old woman's answer was in the negative. She had made up her mind not to give that message from Toni. Then Nick interrogated the houseboy and asked him the same question.

The boy answered:

'No, Monsieur. She was in the drawing-room with the gentleman who called. I haven't seen her since then.'

'Who called? What was his name?'

'I don't know, Monsieur. He didn't give any name?'

'Was it Monsieur Soutro?'

The boy spread out a hand.

'I am sorry, Monsieur, I don't know Monsieur Soutro.'

Nick cursed under his breath and went back to the sitting-room. Obviously Toni's visitor had been Soutro. Nobody else would walk unannounced into the house, and she knew nobody else. Yet Toni had assured him this morning that she never wished to see Soutro again and had given her word on it. Well, this time he would deal with Mr. Soutro! If he could find him!

There was cold hatred in his heart when at length he had started up the Packard and steered it out of the garage in the direction of Soutro's estate. If the fellow had been fool enough to take Toni there, he would pay for it! It was only two minutes' run through the velvet darkness to the neighbouring house.

He found Soutro's villa in darkness save for one solitary light in a downstairs room. Nick switched off his engine. Walking to the verandah, he paused outside the lighted window. It was partially opened. He listened for a moment, his breath quickening. He could hear a man's low voice followed by a woman's smothered laugh.

A woman's laugh! So Toni *was* here! The little fool!

He stood immovable for a moment, a hot gust of rage shaking him. He would not trust himself to go into that room. If he found Toni in Soutro's arms . . .

Soutro—come out here,' he said, in a loud violent voice.

There was a sudden silence. Then he heard Soutro's voice.

'Who the devil is that?'

There was the sound of footsteps on a

polished floor. Then the window opened wide and Garry Soutro came out on to the verandah.

The two men stared at each other.

'Good God—Brendon!' exclaimed Soutro.

A shaft of light from the window fell across his face. Nick fancied that he looked pale and frightened.

'Yes, Soutro,' he said grimly, 'you've gone too far this time. Tell my wife to come out of that room. Then I'll attend to you.'

Soutro stared again, then broke into a laugh.

'My dear fellow, you're crazy! Mrs. Brendon is not here. Why should—'

'Don't lie,' broke in Nick. 'You took her away before, and now—'

'Brendon, don't be a fool. She isn't here, I tell you.'

'Let me into that room.'

'I'm damned if I will. You can't come up here and break into my house—'

He got no further.

Nick swung up his arm and hit Soutro across the face. Then he pushed him aside.

'Get out of my way.'

Soutro, wiping a bruised lip, stood aside, shrugging his shoulders—Brendon was a lunatic!

Nick walked into the room. For a moment he was blinded by the strong light. Then, looking round he saw a girl sitting on the arm

138

of a sofa, swinging long slim legs. A dark-haired girl in a blue chiffon evening dress.

Nick recognized her at once. She was the wife of an American who was a member of the English Club. Bill Young's wife—Valerie. She gave him an angry, resentful look.

'Is this the way you usually call?'

Nick bowed.

'I beg your pardon,' he said coldly; 'I'm afraid I've made a mistake. Good night!'

The girl did not answer. Her face was sulky. She disliked the interruption of her *tête-à-tête*.

'I apologize, Soutro. I am afraid I took things for granted. But I hope it hasn't spoilt your party.'

Soutro wiped a speck of blood from his mouth before he spoke.

'I'm not accepting your apology, Brendon. I treated your wife decently because I felt sorry for her. If she's left you, you have only your fool-self to blame. You can't come here, assaulting a fellow like this. Now get out.'

Nick did not reply. Toni was not with Soutro. That was all he wanted to know. But where was she? Where had she gone?

A troubled, uneasy feeling gripped him. He wondered if he had driven her by his callousness, to some desperate measure.

He spent the rest of the night searching Mentone and Monte Carlo. He went into every hotel, every café and the Casino. There was no trace of her. At one moment he thought of telephoning Helena to ask if she had heard any news. But he knew that would be madness. Helena was the last person with whom Toni would get in touch.

It was almost dawn before he returned to his own house. He felt haggard, exhausted after his futile search. He was too tired to sleep, his nerves would not let him rest. He walked out on to the verandah. There was nothing to be done now but wait, watching the ethereal beauty of the dawn.

It was not until after breakfast that he decided to speak to Helena. She would not be able to help him but she would be somebody to talk to someone at least who *knew* Toni.

'Toni's disappeared,' he told Helena over the telephone. 'Yes, last night. God knows what's happened to her.'

At the other end of the line, Helena listened, her heart beating violently. She spoke kindly and with sympathy, but her eyes were bright with triumph. Black had done his work! It was rather awful, but she consoled herself with the fact that Toni would, in the long run, be better away from Nick, earning her living. By the end of three months she would have sufficient money with which to return to England.

'That's odd, Nick,' she said, keeping the eagerness out of her voice. 'But I expect Toni's all right. You know she wanted a job. She's probably heard of something and will write you when she's settled. You're not worried, are you?'

He tried to make his voice sound natural.

'Surely she wouldn't go off and get a job at night, like that. Still, as you say, she's more than capable of looking after herself.'

'Of course she is. You don't need to worry. I'll jump into a car and come up to you. We'll talk it all over.'

And Helena hung up the receiver before Nick had time to refuse. This was the opportunity for which she had waited, for which she had risked the gamble with Victor Black.

At ten o'clock she was at Cap Martin. She was sweet and sympathetic with Nick and he appeared glad of her company. But in spite of her triumph at her success, Helena was shocked by his appearance. His face was ghastly. His eyes heavy through lack of sleep. She hated to admit even to herself that he was still in love with Toni. But that truth was nevertheless outstanding.

'Unless Toni got a lift in a car, I can't think how she got away so quickly,' he said, refusing to talk to Helena of anything else. 'It takes an hour to walk to the town. I would have passed her after I left you if she'd been walking.'

'You would have done,' Helena agreed. 'But do stop worrying, my dear. You don't surely want Toni any more. She's ruined all our lives.

You can't forget that!'

Nick sighed. He had not forgotten the misery that Toni had caused him or Helena. It was natural that Helena should be bitter. He, too, was bitter. But he could not get rid of the uneasy sensation that he had driven Toni from the house. She was so young, so lovely, and if anything should happen to her . . .

'Let's sit down and smoke quietly and try to forget our mutual worries, Nick,' Helena suggested. 'There's nothing we can do about Toni for the present.'

He tried to smile, to be congenial.

'I'm sorry, Helena. I'm a rotten host. As you say there is nothing we can do but wait and see if Toni turns up again.'

He lit her cigarette. They sat together, smoking in silence for a while. He reflected: It was decent of Helena to come up this morning. He did not want to appear ungrateful. He remembered that it was not the first time she had tried to help him. Her dark eyes were full of sympathy and understanding when she spoke. Nick found it comforting to sit here and listen to her voice, telling him not to worry, assuring him that Toni could take care of herself. When Nick next spoke, it was to reproach himself.

'Perhaps I've been a bit hard on Toni. She was young and very foolish and—'

'Foolish!' repeated Helena, interrupting him. 'That's being lenient, Nick. You know the

142

circumstances under which she got here. It was criminal.'

He stirred uneasily. Why was it that he hated hearing one word against Toni? Yet he could not deny, even to himself, that she had been a liar and a cheat.

'Oh well!' he said, 'it's no good slanging her. You might as well slang me, Helena. Yes, why don't you say things to me. I wasn't very loyal to you, I was ready to believe Toni's story and then—'

Helena interrupted him again. She wanted to show herself in beautiful colours of generosity and understanding.

'Don't reproach yourself, Nick. Toni was so clever about it all—I honestly don't blame you for being so beguiled and misled. And out here it was lonely for you—Toni was pretty—and there you are.'

He have her a brief smile.

'You make me feel more than ever ashamed, my dear.'

She gave him a long, intense look.

'You ought to know by now how much you mean to me, Nick.'

But he was not ready for that—yet. She could see how he shied from it. She knew enough about men not to make the mistake of pitching herself at his head today. He was raw about Toni. Gradually, very gradually, she would smooth him down, and make him realize it would be better for him to put Toni right out of his life, and dream again that dream of love which she—Helena—had shared with him in their early days together.

Helena was not only a consummate actress but a past-mistress in the art of deceiving herself. Quite blithely she forgot how hardly she had behaved to Nick; how she had neglected him; how fully she had intended shelving him altogether for Bobby. Now that he was a prize to be won again, she remembered only the first days of her engagement to him. She even began to feel that Toni had done her a real wrong in coming out here.

She touched on the subject of the dissolution of Toni's marriage with Nick.

'You won't want to go on being tied to her now, will you, Nick? You see how little she cares for you—she's walked out on you again. For your pride's sake, you'll want a divorce, won't you?'

He turned from her so she could not see the look in his eyes. He felt that he was dead, empty of all emotion. Yet his nerves were so overstrung that the emotional side of him was waiting to flare up at a touch. Not a touch from Helena, but from Toni. If she had only really loved him—how much he could have forgiven her—and how he loathed the thought of divorce, and of flinging all the passionate love they had shared into the void.

When he answered Helena he tried to speak

lightly:

'Yes, I suppose I'll have to get a divorce.'

She bit her lip in sudden excitement. That was a concession. If she waited for the right moment, she would get back her man. She was sure of it.

'And once you've settled things with Toni, will you stay on at the farm?'

He shrugged his shoulders.

'I suppose so. I'm interested in my work.'

'Don't you think a change of scene would do you good? Why not come back to England with me?'

He shifted uneasily from one foot to another.

'I don't think I could, Helena. I couldn't leave the farm without a manager.'

'You could get one. Honestly, Nick, it would do you good to see London again.'

He sighed and walked to the window and looked across the garden into the distance. The golden day was still. From the pens he could hear the barking of foxes. He had said that he was interested in his work. That was no longer true. He was interested in nothing. Between these two women, Toni and Helena, he felt curiously wrecked and alone. Helena was talking about town—their old haunts, the good times they used to have. The new places that she could show him. They used to dance together. Why shouldn't they dance again and make up for lost time? And so on, until his mind teemed with the idea of living in London again. But into the picture persistently came Toni . . . Toni with her large eyes drenched in tears, beseeching him to believe in her. How he had loved her.

He turned back to Helena, struggling with himself.

'I'll have to think things over, my dear. But I certainly couldn't get away from Cap Martin until I found someone to take charge for me. My herd-boy's good, but not good enough. They all need discipline.'

Helena fancied that it might be discreet of her to 'talk shop' with him.

'Is the farm paying handsomely these days?'

'Quite.'

'Do you know you've never taken me down to see the farm. I should be thrilled—'

'That reminds me,' broke in Nick suddenly, 'one of my best vixens has just had a new litter and been very ill. We had a cub in here last night—trying to save it—'

He called loudly for Marie.

She came running in.

'Yes, Monsieur.'

'Where's that cub Pierre brought in last night?'

'Taken back to the kennels this morning, Monsieur.'

Nick gave an exclamation of anger.

'Who the devil gave you that order? Pierre must have known it would die if it were left with the others.'

The old French woman looked at her master with astonishment. She had never known him to speak to her like that before. But, of course, *le pauvre*! . . . Madame had left him. He was feeling wretchedly unhappy. She looked with hostility at the tall dark English girl who was with him. This was no friend of poor little Madame's. She was the cause of all the trouble, Marie was certain of it.

Nick said to Helena:

'There you are! They do damn fool things like that unless I'm on the spot. Toni and I nursed that cub for an hour last night. Spoon-fed it with brandy and milk and kept it in a blanket, and they take it back to the kennels!'

'Was it a valuable one?'

'No. It would never have much of a coat, not what we call a rough, bright skin.'

'Then why worry?'

He did not answer. But even in the chaos of his mind he had the reaction that Toni was a kinder, more human person than Helena. Helena had such a mercenary streak. That had always been a fault of hers. She would only trouble to save the cub if the pelt were worthwhile. That was not very attractive of her. But Toni, last night on her knees beside the basket, had administered to the sick cub as though it were a baby.

He drew a hand across his eyes. Damn, *damn*, the thought of Toni. Why couldn't he forget her? If Helena was hard, so much the better. Hard people got on in this world. It was no good being a soft fool—as soft as he had been about Toni when he had first fallen in love with her.

Deliberately he put an arm round Helena's shoulder and said:

'Let's have a drink and then you shall taste one of Marie's omelettes. It was darn decent of you to come up here this morning. You ought to have a grudge against me—but you don't appear to have, and I'm grateful.'

That was enough to set her heart beating faster. As she walked with him towards the dining-room she thought:

'Fortune smiled on me last night when I met that old reprobate—Victor Black. I rather think Toni's day is over and that mine is beginning again.'

But there, Helena made a mistake. Nick was being non-committal. He was putting up a bluff for Helena. He was not prepared to let her see how much he felt Toni's disappearance. But underneath he was as determined now to find Toni again as he had been the last time she had left him, with Soutro. And that thought grew and grew until it superceded every other one in his mind.

The afternoon dragged. At tea-time he excused himself from Helena.

'I've got to do some work, my dear. You'd better let the man drive you back to your hotel.'

But Helena was impatient. She pleaded to be allowed to remain.

Nick grew suddenly cold. He was sick of Helena and her sympathy. He was conscious of nothing but the gnawing need for Toni. Toni who was his wife. With every hour that passed he grew more convinced that he had driven her away by his stupidity, and that whatever she had done in the beginning when she had come out here in Helena's place, she was fundamentally good. She *must* be. Could he forget the look in her eyes when she held that sick cub in her arms. A look that might have been there for a child of hers—*and his*!

Raw with nerves, he snapped at Helena:

'I want to be left alone!'

Helena's feelings got the better of her. Her vanity was hurt and she knew, instinctively, that the shadow of Toni was between them. She was so infuriated that her hatred and jealousy sprang forth, thereby putting the nail in the coffin of her own ambitions concerning Nick.

'You're a fool, Nick!' she said, her cheeks crimson, her eyes hot with rage, 'you're letting the thought of Toni come between us.'

Then Nick froze altogether.

'My dear Helena,' he said. He spoke in a voice that made her heart sink. She saw too late what she had done. Once before, in England, they had quarrelled. He had spoken in the same icy voice and it had taken her days to bring him back to a lover-like mood. 'My dear girl, I don't think there's any question of Toni coming between us at this precise moment. I'm afraid she achieved that weeks ago. I admit that I did you a wrong when I believed what Toni had to say, and married her. But nothing gives you the right to dictate to me. I won't be dictated to by anybody.'

Then Helena's anger broke out afresh.

'I like that! You ought to be on your knees to me—shelving me the way you did.'

He broke in.

'I'm not going to be nagged at. I'm not in the mood to stand it. You have right on your side. So have I. So, for all we know, has Toni. It'll work itself out. Meanwhile I think you'd better go back to your hotel and leave things alone.'

Helena trembled violently. She felt almost sick with disappointment.

'To let that little— come between us! . . .'

She used a word that made Nick raise his brows. He gave her a not very pleasant smile.

'My dear! This isn't going to become a brawl, is it?'

Speechlessly she turned and picked up her bag and hat. He watched her without a vestige of emotion. Never before had the hard, coarse streak in Helena been more apparent. He knew that whatever happened between him and Toni, he would never care for Helena again. He even found himself playing with the crazy thought that perhaps Toni had spoken the truth and that Helena *had* written that original letter, believing that she was about to make a better marriage in London. But he did not dwell on such an idea. He only knew that he wanted to get Helena out of his house and readjust his life—and Toni's—in his own way.

When he put Helena in the car he said good-bye politely. So politely that she blenched, for somehow she knew that this was the end.

Still shivering with a rage that she tried to repress, she said:

'Perhaps when you realize that what I called your precious Toni was justified, you'll ask me up again,' she said, swallowing hard.

He looked her straight in her eyes.

'I think not, Helena. If it's all the same to you, I'll put the money for your return ticket to England in an envelope this evening and post it to you.'

'You'll be sorry for this.'

'I'm sorry already—for everything. But not particularly for this,' he said.

Then he turned and walked back into the house.

The chauffeur steered the car out of the drive and on to the road leading to Mentone, and Helena stared blankly before her, wondering how she could have been such a colossal fool as to lose her self-control—and incidentally lose Nick Brendon for ever.

She was fully aware of the fact that if she had been what the world would call 'sporting', she would have told Nick where to find his wife—told him about Black and San Remo. But she had no intention of doing that. Let Nick sing for his wife! Let him find her if he could. She was furious with him—with Toni— and most of all with herself.

CHAPTER TWELVE

Toni remembered little about the drive to San Remo with Victor Black. She realized that they were taking the coast road. It was the same road which she had taken with Nick when they had gone to Italy together. When they came to the frontier she recognized the officer who had examined their passports. She remembered what Nick had said.

'These fellows have an eye for a pretty woman.'

She tried to forget the details of that day. They were too closely connected with the misery which had followed. Now she was going to put it all behind her. She had a job. In a few weeks she would be returning to England and pick up the threads of her old life.

Victor Black seemed to know every street in San Remo. He steered the car through a maze of tram-lines. Then suddenly, he pulled up outside a brightly-lit house in a busy quarter of the town.

'Here we are,' he said. 'Let me take your bag.'

She followed him into the building. He took a bunch of keys from his pocket and opened a door in the hall. They were in a small well-furnished room. There was a desk in the corner. The walls were covered with signed photographs.

'Is this your office?'

He nodded.

'Yes. This is where I work. I'll take you into the dance-room now and introduce you to the girls. You'll need to have a quick rehearsal if you're going to dance tonight.'

'Do you think I'll manage it?'

'Sure you will. I'll tell Florry to run over the number with you. Then come back here to see me.'

He took Toni's arm and led her along a narrow passage. On the floor in the next room a crowd of girls were tap-dancing. A gramophone played a noisy French tune. The girls wore silk shirts and shorts. They stopped dancing when Toni came in and clustered round her, staring at her inquisitively. They all spoke at once. Toni stared back at them blankly. One spoke to her in French, one in Italian. She understood nothing until a tall fair-haired girl pushed her way forward.

'You're English, aren't you?' she asked.

'Yes.'

'Going to work here?'

Toni smiled.

'I hope so. Mr. Black is giving me a chance. But I'm a little nervous. I've never done any cabaret work before.'

'Don't worry about that. The work's easy enough. You'll soon get the hang of it. Just keep on the right side of Florry.'

'Who is Florry?' Toni asked.

'Black's wife. She more or less runs this place. She's a devil to work for. Anyone would think us girls were a troupe of circus ponies.'

Toni laughed.

'I bet she thinks I'm pretty dense. I don't suppose I'll know what she's talking about.'

The girl winked at Toni.

'Here she comes. Good luck! I'm off.'

Toni saw a big, heavily-built woman, with dyed red hair crossing the room towards her. She wore a black evening dress, with a silver-fox cape thrown over her shoulders. She had a haggard, disillusioned face which must once have been beautiful. Toni concentrated on the fur cape. Silver foxes! How the sight of them hurt. She could see the little cub which Nick had given her to nurse. And all the other lithe, graceful creatures, bounding and barking in their pens. How horrible it was to think of them being put to death no matter how humanely and those glorious skins torn from

154

their bodies. Of course she was much too tender-hearted to be married to a man who ran a fox-farm for a living!

Nick was tender-hearted too at times. He had been so very gentle with that cub. And once, so very gentle with her. Oh Nick, *Nick!* Fresh agony tore at Toni. The woman wearing the fur cape was looking her up and down. In a strident voice she said:

'Are you the new girl?'

Toni nodded.

'Yes. Mr. Black has just brought me here. He wants me to try to dance tonight. But I'm afraid I may find it difficult. I'm out of practice.'

'You certainly look tired. Are you ill?'

'No. I'll be all right in a few minutes.'

Florry shrugged her shoulders.

'Come along. then. I'll see what I can do with you.'

She led Toni to the far end of the room and, changing the record on the gramophone, told her to listen.

'That's the number you'll be doing tonight. Follow my steps.'

Toni tried to concentrate on the woman's movements, but she knew she was doing badly. She felt sick and her head was swimming. She found it difficult to follow the music, to hear what Florry was saying. She was about to stop, to say that she could not go on, when she heard a voice behind her. It was Victor Black.

155

'That's fine,' he said. 'You'll be all right tonight—after you've had a rest. Come into my office. I want you to sign the contract. See you later, Florry.'

Toni followed him like an automaton. She was only half-conscious of what was going on around her. Black shut the door of his office. The sound of the music and of the girls' chattering voices died away.

The atmosphere of Black's office was thick with cigar smoke. Toni sank into a chair and drew a hand across her eyes.

'I'm afraid it was hopeless. I'm so tired.'

Black laughed.

'Nonsense, baby, don't worry your pretty head. You'll be grand tonight.'

He crossed to a glass and chromium table on which stood a tray of drinks, and a box of Turkish cigarettes. He poured a stiff brandy-and-soda into a glass and handed it to Toni.

'Swallow this. It'll make you feel better.'

She took the glass and sipped the cognac, glad of its warmth. She certainly did need a stimulant.

'What about the contract?' Toni asked.

'That can wait. I merely mentioned it to get you away from Florry. She's jealous of every young girl I bring here. I admit she has cause this time.'

Toni threw him a quick, nervous glance and set down her brandy.

'What do you mean?'

156

'I'm flattering you, baby, I mean that you're the loveliest blonde we've ever had in the show. That's why I intend to look after you myself. You're fresh as a daisy, my dear. The rest of 'em are tired orchids.' He chuckled, pleased with his own simile.

'Look after me yourself,' Toni repeated dully.

He sat down on the arm of her chair.

'Yes, my dear. You're too good to mix with the others,' he said, trying to take her hand.

Toni hardly heard what he said. She only knew that the touch of his hand revolted her, that she wanted to get out of the room.

She said:

'I must go now.'

She heard Victor Black laugh. He put out a hand, touched her golden hair.

'You're beautiful,' he whispered. 'Beautiful, baby.'

Toni moved away, her heart pounding with sudden fear.

'Don't be a swine! Let me out of here.'

He looked nervously around him.

'Ssh—little idiot. Florry will hear you. Be sensible. Listen now, Blondie! . . .'

He tried to catch her arm.

A blind rage swept her. She raised her hand and hit him across the face. Her hand smashed against his horn-rimmed spectacles and the glass splintered. With an oath he let her go and put a shaking hand up to his eyes.

'You damned little fool! You've broken my glasses and you might have blinded me.'

He stood there, livid with anger. He took off the bent rims and blinked at her short-sightedly. A piece of the glass had cut his forehead and it began to bleed. He was wiping it with his handkerchief when the door opened, and his wife walked in. She stopped for a moment when she saw him.

'Say! What's the matter? What's happened?'

The colour spread darkly across his cheeks.

'Oh nothing much. I hit my face against the door. My glasses broke.'

The woman's eyes narrowed. Her face was alive with jealousy and suspicion. She did not trust her husband. She knew that he was tired of her! She held him in contempt. But in her particular fashion she cared for him. He was her man and she had suffered for and through him. She turned to Toni.

'You'd better come with me. You've got work to do.'

She led Toni away to the room where the others were practising their new steps. She was certain that Victor had made a fool of himself. The girl looked scared to death. But she felt no particular pity for Toni, only for herself. She was miserable, jealous. She knew she could no longer hold her husband. She was too old and *passé*.

'Get over with the rest,' she said harshly,

'and learn your steps. You'll find it no harder than entertaining my husband.'

The next hour was a nightmare to Toni. She found herself lined up with half-a-dozen other girls. She tried to dance, to follow the instructions which Florry gave her. She felt giddy, breathless. Mechanically, she obeyed orders, moved, kept time to the music.

When the rehearsal was finished she sat down with the troupe for supper. They were a cheerful crowd. They laughed and gossiped in many languages. They discussed their sweethearts, their triumphs and disappointments, quite openly. They saw that Toni was depressed and tried to cheer her up.

'I expect you're homesick,' the English girl said. 'I was too. But you'll like San Remo. There's plenty to do during the day—tennis and swimming.'

'I'm sure there is,' Toni tried to smile back. 'I'll be fine tomorrow.'

She hoped that the girls would leave her alone until she had time to pull herself together. She knew that her powers of resistance were almost at an end. She was in a curiously lethargic state of mind and body. She had no desire to move. It was as if she had lost her will-power. The nasty little scene with Victor Black had been the final blow to her overwrought nerves.

Like ghosts, like flickering shadows of a dream, there chased across her mind the remembrance of other scenes. The memory of a man with a thin brown face and blue eyes. Dim, painful memories of the agony of a helpless love; of the cruelty of it all. After that there were no more visions. Only dull blankness, a sense of hopelessness.

She was dressed that night in a dress of silver lamé. It was sewn with shimmering blue sequins. It clung tightly to her figure. Her arms and legs were bare. She wore high-heeled silver sandals, showing her scarlet lacquered toenails, and a silver Juliet cap with iridescent wings at each side. There were glittering, transparent wings attached to her shoes.

They told her that she was a Dragon-Fly.

'That was the Dragon-Fly dance I showed you,' Florry said. 'Try to remember what I told you to do.'

Toni made no reply. She looked at herself in the mirror in her dressing-room. She found the slim, glittering figure unreal. It did not seem that it was Toni at all. She thought she looked dreadful. Her face, she knew, was dead white underneath the heavy, vivid make-up.

She sat huddled in a chair waiting for the ordeal which was before her. She would probably make a fool of herself. But she did not care. All she wanted was to be good enough to hold down her job, to make some money, then get back to London.

She could hear the throb of the band. The hum of conversation from the dance-floor.

One of the girls was crooning a sentimental song in a deep, husky voice. She appeared to be popular. There was a burst of applause when she stopped.

A few minutes later there came a knock on her door. Victor Black entered and closed the door behind him. He seemed to have forgotten the scene with her. He was smiling, politely.

'We're just about ready for you,' he said. 'Don't worry. You're going to be a success.'

'I hope so.'

He gave a look at her shimmering sequin dress.

'You look great. You'll be a riot. You can hardly wonder that I lost my head this evening. But forget about that. There's work to be done now.'

It was one o'clock when Toni went on to the floor. For a moment she felt dazed by the blinding limelight which played on her. She barely saw the figures at the tables around her. She only knew that the band was playing, that she must dance. She began to move automatically to the rhythm of the music. She turned and twisted on her silver-winged feet. She tried to remember what Florry had told her. The Dragon-Fly must be graceful, sparkling and swiftly beautiful.

Victor Black, watching from the back of the room, felt he had reason to congratulate himself. He could tell that Toni was being a success. He could sense the admiration and delight of the men in the crowd. He, himself, had never seen a figure or a face quite as lovely as Toni's. She was perfect as she poised on her little silver feet, the iridescent wings glittering in her cap, the lovely lines of her figure revealed by the strong light.

The people in that club were a strange mixture. Men and women of all nationalities came here to drink and dance and watch the Cabaret. And tonight an American and his wife had driven across the frontier in their big powerful car for an evening's amusement.

The man was William Young, a member of the English Club in Mentone. When Toni first began to dance he was interested in her only as any man is interested in a young and lovely girl. But after a moment, staring through the smoke-laden atmosphere, he gave a low whistle and turned to his wife.

'Gee, Val! That's no ordinary blonde. Shall I tell you who she is?'

Valerie Young bored and dissatisfied, and still in love with Garry Soutro, yawned.

'Who?' she asked.

'Mrs. Nicholas Brendon. I've seen her with Brendon once or twice, you know, Val. All kinds of wild stories have been circulated about her.'

Mrs. Young sat up.

Mrs. Brendon, eh? That was interesting. Why, heavens! she remembered that night in Garry's bungalow when Nick Brendon turned up, thinking she was his wife. She hoped to see Garry before long and tell him. He wasn't in Mentone at the moment. He had had to go over to London to his father who was dying. He might not be back for a month, but when he came back . . . this would be a piece of news.

She stared at the Dragon-Fly. The girl's face was so thickly coated with paint, it looked like a lovely mask.

'You're quite sure, Bill?'

'Positive. That means there's been trouble between Brendon and his wife, and she's got a job here. Pretty lousy work for an English girl.'

'Say, let's send for the manager and ask if we can speak to her,' suggested Valerie Young.

But when Victor Black came to the table occupied by the American couple, he had no intention of allowing them, or anybody else, to talk to his new dancer. She had been a crashing success. The boys were howling for an encore now. He wasn't going to have her enticed away from him by some American manager. So he bowed and apologized. He regretted the fair-haired dancer wasn't available. The moment she finished dancing here she had to leave the place and go on to one of the other dance-clubs where she would give another show.

There was not a vestige of truth in it, but the Youngs had to be satisfied. Bill Young even began to fear that he had made a mistake.

Possibly the girl wasn't Mrs. Brendon, after all. But Valerie Young, intrigued by the idea, determined to pass that piece of news on to Garry Soutro when he came back to the South.

Unfortunately for Toni it was a good month before the news was delivered to the man who had befriended her. Four weeks of bitter loneliness and hard work and the feeling that life was not worth living, before Soutro proved himself once again a friend.

For Soutro, more than intrigued by what his latest love told him, took the trouble to make enquiries and heard that Brendon was living alone out at his farm, and that his wife had disappeared in mysterious circumstances.

Soutro had no particular liking for Nick Brendon. He owed him a grudge for that cut across the cheek which had been delivered to him, the night when Brendon had called at his villa. On the other hand, he liked Toni. He felt that she was being given a rotten deal. And if she was in that troupe at San Remo, Brendon ought to know it.

So, one night when Nick was sitting alone wondering if he would ever trace Toni, a telephone call came through for him. A call from the last man from whom he expected to hear.

The moment he recognized Soutro's voice, hope set Nick Brendon's heart beating madly. He could surely count on this being news— news of Toni at last.

Soutro said:

'I really don't care a damn whether you're eating your heart out, Brendon, but I don't like to think of your wife in a lousy troupe dancing in a night club at San Remo.'

Nick was staggered.

'Where in God's name did you get that information from?' he asked tensely.

'Friends of mine,' was the cautious answer, 'they saw her there. Of course they may be mistaken, but you might like to run over and see for yourself.'

'Look here, Soutro,' began Nick, 'I'm grateful for this.'

'I don't want your gratitude,' came back the curt answer, 'and if you don't mind me saying so, you're a fool. That wife of yours is in love with you, and always has been. Why aren't you more grateful to her?'

Soutro rang off.

For a moment Nicholas Brendon stood there, his whole body shaking with excitement. If Soutro was right—if those friends of his were right—he would have Toni back in this house tonight. He would bring her back, not with brutality or by force, but with the tenderness which he had so long denied her. Soutro was right. He *had* been a fool. The worst kind of idiot, deluded by a woman. And that woman, Helena. had given the whole show away in a letter written to him from London a fortnight ago. Not a pretty letter;

not one written in any desire to make amends. Just a piece of insolence and revenge.

She had never loved him, she had said. Toni had been quite right when she had told him that she, Helena, was sick of him and wanted to make a better marriage. And she was making that marriage right now. She had found a South American—a diamond merchant—who was not particular about her past, and was only too keen to take her with him to Brazil. Before sailing, she thought that Nick might like to know she hadn't missed anything by letting Toni step into her shoes.

A coarse, hateful letter which had made Nick loathe the thought that he had ever meant to make Helena his wife. But at least he could bless her for writing it. For it cleared Toni so absolutely. He knew now that every word Toni had told him was true, and that all Helena's stories had been false. A fool, Soutro had just called him. But he was worse than that. He was a monster. He had behaved monstrously to that slip of a child, who had bought her way out here for no other reason than that she had loved him in the highest and most romantic sense.

If it were only true that she was dancing in San Remo . . . Heavens, if only it were true, and he could find her, and beg her to start life with him again!

He flung on a coat and rushed out to the garage to start up his car.

CHAPTER THIRTEEN

For six weeks now, Toni had been performing the Dragon-Fly dance which, in its way, had become quite famous.

Black was so satisfied with the money which she drew to his club he no longer pestered her with his personal attentions. But his wife had never forgotten the fact that he had had an eye on the girl, and she did what she could to make Toni's life a misery. Added to which, her triumph bred petty jealousies and spite among the rest of the troupe.

The life she led was barely tolerable. The applause from the crowd after her dance every night, meant nothing to her. She had only one desire—to get away from this dancing hell, back to England where she could lead a normal, wholesome life. Where she could shut out the mere memory of the Mediterranean. She had chosen it. She had come here believing that she could make something of a life with Nicholas Brendon. And she had failed. Everything had gone wrong. She only endured the unattractive position in which she now found herself, strengthened by the knowledge that her little heap of savings was growing steadily week by week.

When she thought of Nick, she tried to hate him. But she couldn't. She could remember him only with love and anguish, trying to blot out visions of him installing Helena in her place.

That she was still his wife gave her little consolation. She had long since pawned her wedding ring, adding the money towards the fare which she wanted for home. That he would, in time, divorce her, she had no doubt. And meanwhile the summer sped by, the days and nights grew hotter, the work harder and a new trouble dogged her footsteps.

Her health was failing. She seemed to have no vitality. At the end of a night's dancing, she was drenched with sweat and so done that she could not move or speak for an hour. And she was losing weight; looking ghastly when the powder and paint were removed from her face.

That wasn't pleasing Victor Black or Florry. They did not want the new blonde to lose her looks. But they made life no easier for her. She was kept at her job, and made to dance, whether she was ill or well.

Came the night when she fainted in the middle of the dance. The watching audience thought for a moment that it was all part of the cabaret when the Dragon-Fly stumbled and fell, a little glittering heap on the floor.

Then when she did not get up again, the music faltered and stopped. Victor Black came running forward and bent over her.

You can't do this. You'll ruin me. Get up,

168

you little fool . . .'

He whispered the words under pretence of lifting her to her feet. She was only half-conscious, but one thing penetrated her brain and kept her from sinking back into oblivion. Another voice which seemed to come from a long distance. A very English, well-remembered and beloved voice that said:

'Damn you. Let her go. Give her to me at once!'

She gave a little cry:

'Nick! *Nick!*'

Black stared impudently at the tall Englishman with the thin brown face and blue eyes, blazing with rage.

'Who the hell are you?' Black began.

'My name's Brendon, and this girl is my wife,' was the answer, 'now get out.'

And Victor Black got out. He was too experienced to tackle an outraged husband. It was just his luck that Toni had been followed and found. Cursing roundly, he gave the band an order to start up the next number.

When Toni came fully back to her senses again, she realized that she was being carried in Nick's arms out of the club, into the soft Italian night. In her glittering dress she lay against him like a broken toy. She had not the strength to speak for a long while. She just put her head on his shoulder and wondered, while the tears crept down her cheeks, why he was being so kind to her.

He found a big rug in the car and wrapped it around her. Then a flask of brandy which he drew from his pocket, uncorked, and held to her lips.

'Just a little of this, my sweet. It will pull you together.'

She asked herself if this was all a dream. '*My sweet.*' He had not called her that for so long, and never with such a note in his voice. There was nothing left of the cold, inhuman man who had bullied her and driven her away from him. He was the Nick whom she had adored for so long, and whom she had married . . . when was it? . . . it seemed an eternity ago.

When the brandy had warmed and strengthened her, she whispered: 'How did you find me?'

'Never mind that now,' he answered, 'I'll tell you later. I want to get you back home. God! how thin you are! You poor little thing.'

'Where is Helena?' she began.

'Don't mention that name to me, Toni. She's gone. And I'll tell you all about that later. Let this be enough for the moment . . . I know the truth, and I don't deserve to be forgiven. But I didn't know. I was a blind fool and I just ask you to forgive me, because I realize now that I couldn't bear life without you any more.'

She was still under the impression that this could only be a heavenly dream. A strange feeling of rest, of *rightness*, stole over her as she huddled under the rug in the big Packard, and felt his arm about her, and his lips against her hand.

She whispered:

'Oh, Nick . . . I couldn't have borne it without you any more, either.'

'Darling,' he said, and covered both her hands with wild, remorseful kisses, 'let's get away from here. Let's get back to our home quickly . . . as quickly as we can!'

That drive home was the most extraordinary experience for Toni. Nick drove 'all out' along the white, dusty road which wound like a silver ribbon under the moon, across the Italian frontier, into Cap Martin again. Neither of them spoke. There was so much to say, yet so little to be said. So many explanations to be given, yet none necessary. They had found each other again, and they both felt as though they were not in this world, but another of their own making.

Like a nightmare stretched behind Toni that other world in which she had lived for six weeks in Victor Black's troupe. And like a bad dream for Nick, the memory of those long weeks of loneliness and self-reproach that had followed her disappearance from the farm.

Dawn was breaking when, at length, the big throbbing car drew up before Brendon's house. A rim of orange and vermilion streaked the clear heavenly blue of the Mediterranean sky; a little breeze was shivering in the palm trees, bringing a scent of flowers in its wake.

Nick switched off the engine and looked at his wife. He thought he had never seen anything more tragic than that small pointed face, with its thick smearing of make-up, and the transparency of her small hands and delicate wrists.

'Oh, my darling,' he said, 'I shall never forgive myself for bringing you to this . . .'

He got out of the car, lifted her up in his arms and carried her into the house. His heart sank at the frailty of the thin, light body which he held.

She tried to smile, but could not. Her head sank against his shoulder in an exhausted way and her eyes shut. She murmured his name, and no more.

Then Nicholas Brendon knew what fear was. He wondered if he had found her too late—if that young, brave heart which he had broken was beyond mending, this night.

He hurried with her into the house, carried her up to her bedroom, calling for Marie, and for the boy to light the fires at once.

Marie, waddling in her dressing-gown, answered her master's voice, none too pleased that Madame had returned again. There had been peace in the house for the last six weeks, although she was forced to admit that Monsieur looked like a ghost and had eaten none of her best dishes.

When she saw her young mistress stretched

on the bed looking so ill, so piteous, the mother-instinct in her conquered petty jealousy. With many exclamations of horror, she set to work to bring Madame back to life.

Some hours later Toni, lying blissfully in warm blankets on her own bed, a wood fire crackling in the grate, dispelling the coolness of the early morning, realized that this was no dream but an exquisite reality.

She was home again. The horror of the past was wiped out. Nick was wiping it out, by all that he had to say as he sat there beside her, pouring out his heart.

'I must have been crazy to take Helena's word against yours,' he said, not once, but many times, 'I see now that it was she who was the liar and the cheat, and not you, my darling.'

'But I did wrong,' she said, his hand holding fast to hers, 'I had no right to give her that money and bribe her to let me come out here to you.'

'You came to me because you loved me. I know it now and I realize how utterly undeserved that love was, Toni,' he said.

She gave a long sigh.

'If you really believe that's why I came out here, I don't mind anything, Nick.'

'I do believe it, Toni. I ask you from the bottom of my heart to forgive me for everything. I was an unutterable brute. It makes me shudder to think how vilely I

173

behaved.'

She shook her head.

'You mustn't feel that way. You were in a frightful position. You had no reason to doubt Helena and, on the surface, every reason to doubt me.'

He wondered why women were so forgiving . . . women like Toni. And he wondered how he could ever have disbelieved one word she said, when he looked at her now.

The clear morning light showed up a very different Toni from the one whom he had rescued from San Remo last night. The tragic Dragon-Fly had vanished. Marie had wiped the mess of paint from her face. The silky fair hair had been brushed back from her forehead and tied with a ribbon. Her face, very thin and pinched, was the face of a small child, with enormous eyes. But the eyes were those of a woman who had been through some terrible strain. And it was when he looked into those eyes that Nick felt life would never be long enough for him to show his remorse.

When Soutro's name came up, Nick said:

'I've said a lot against that fellow. And in his way he's no good. But he's been fine about you, and I shall write and tell him so.'

'I think he really knew how much I really loved you, Nick.'

'Everybody seems to have known that, except me,' he said.

He looked so miserable, so like a boy

ashamed of some wrong-doing, instead of the cynical Nick with the devil in him, that she had to laugh for sheer joy that that devil had been driven out.

She patted the bed and said:

'Come here.'

He sat beside her, encircling her slight body with his arms. She put out a hand and smoothed the dark hair back from his forehead.

'I love being here, like this. But I want my honeymoon. Do you realize, Nick, that we never had one?'

'Indeed I do, my sweet. And the moment you're fit, I shall take you over to England. You'd like that, wouldn't you?'

She put her lips to his cheek.

'I'd love it. I used to live in Devonshire when I was a little girl. Cap Martin is full of glamour, but I feel that I'd like my son—to be born in England.'

He drew back from her swiftly, his brown face scarlet and his eyes amazed.

'*Your son!*'

'Ours, my dear. The doctor had a talk with me this morning when you were out of the room. You know, I've been feeling pretty bad for the last few weeks. It wasn't just the dancing, it was . . . well, we'll have a strange sort of honeymoon, Nicky. Sort of getting ready for our child, and it's going to be a boy. Just as handsome as you, but without that

175

devil, I hope.'

He was speechless for a moment. What she had just revealed to him seemed like a miracle. Then he took her back in his arms, whispering crazy, adoring things to her.

'If only I'd known . . . if only I'd known and behaved differently to you. I'm responsible for all your misery and I can hardly bear it, Toni.'

'You don't have to worry about it now, darling.'

'You shall go to England, my sweet. We shall have a cottage in Devonshire and anything in the world that I can give you, my dear, *my dear.*'

She felt enormously happy and content. For a moment she stroked his hair in silence, then she said:

'Do you want to come back here again?'

'Frankly, no. I'd like to sell the farm and start life somewhere else. It reminds me too much of my own brutality.'

'It isn't that, Nick. It's only that I couldn't bear to see the foxes killed. Do you remember that little cub? . . .'

'I could never forget it, Toni. It was when I saw you holding it, that I first had a vision of what you might look like, with a child in your arms.'

'It's all going to come true.'

He kissed her again and stood up, his eyes excited and eager. He was like one intoxicated with happiness.

'Can I go and tell Marie the news?'

'Of course you can.'

'I adore you,' he said irrelevantly, and tore out of the room.

She gave a long sigh, lay back on the pillow and shut her eyes.

She began to dwell on the miraculous thought of her coming child. No doubt a son of hers and Nick's would be sure to have a spice of the devil in him. Well, why not? she reflected drowsily. Nick could be a most *attractive* devil when he chose.

Toni laughed softly to herself, and drifted into sleep.